AN UNDIPLOMATIC MURDER

A RITCHIE AND FITZ SCI-FI MURDER MYSTERY

KATE MACLEOD

1

MURDINA RITCHIE FELT a strange disconnect between the familiar and the unfamiliar.

Everything immediately around her were things she was thoroughly used to. She was pretty sure she'd even been inside this very diner train car on an earlier trip on the intergalactic railway, maybe even the exact same booth.

Certainly, the other cadets in their Oymyakon Foreign Service Academy uniforms were familiar to her, after living in dorms together for over two years now.

Her seat mate in particular, her buddy Antoinette Moreau, was more familiar to Ritchie than even her own family. The bland expression of boredom that never left her face, the topknot of fine whitish-blond hair piled on her head making up a bit for the height she lacked compared to the other cadets, it was all something Ritchie saw every day.

The smells of French fries and flame-grilled meat were so thick in the air Ritchie could feel it starting to coat her hair in oily goodness. The feeling of having just tried to eat her own weight in greasy food, the heavy warmth lingering in her belly, wasn't something she felt every day, but it wasn't unfamiliar.

But the view out of the windows? That was entirely new.

It wasn't what she was acclimated to seeing out a train window, the usual ever present thunderstorms and gray mountainsides of Oymyakon. They had left that behind the day before.

Neither was it the tropical, all ocean and beaches world of Epsilon 20, where she had spent her semester break a year before. She did see a few glittering blue patches of lakes here and there, but nothing big enough for ships.

No, the planet below her was overwhelming covered in green. Trees and meadows, for sure, but mostly elaborately structured gardens, the greenery arranged in patterns that must only be visible from the sky.

And at the heart of every garden, almost as an afterthought, was a cluster of a few buildings, all of creamy marble. Some had blue or pink streaks, others had flecks of black or gold, but most were just a gleaming white that struck a lovely contrast to the greenery crowded all around it.

She was finally seeing Braga, the planet of universities. There were other universities scattered throughout the Union of Free Worlds, of course, but all the important ones were here. Both foreign service branches had their main campus here. So did all the armed forces. There were also schools for fine arts, for business, for science and technology.

It was all completely overwhelming. And Ritchie hadn't even set foot on it yet.

"We're too far north to see Guy's school," Moreau told her. As if that was the only logical reason Ritchie was raptly staring out the window. But then again, very little impressed Moreau. She tended to forget how much of the beautiful side of the universe was still a novelty for Ritchie.

"I know. I've checked the maps," Ritchie said, still with her face pressed up close to the window.

"We have a lot of free periods over the last few days here. I'm sure you'll be able to meet up at least once," Moreau said. Then she laughed. "Guy will make sure of it, anyway."

"I'm sure he will," Ritchie said with a smile. But inside, her heart ached.

She and Guy had spent the entire semester break together, something she hadn't seen coming. But he had been on the train when she left the academy at the end of the semester, and he had taken her on his family's private shuttle directly to the Space Station Delta Delta Nu, where she lived in a single room apartment with her mother and grandmother. He had rented an apartment of his own in the swankier part of the station, a huge suite of rooms all under a glass dome that offered panoramic views of space all around the station. She hadn't even known such places existed on her home station. She had spent nearly every hour of every day there, with Guy.

If he had hoped to spend any time somewhere more interesting than a grungy space station at the edge of the Union, he never said so. In fact, he seemed to genuinely enjoy taking her and her mother and grandmother out to restaurants and theaters and museums, all places that, like his temporary apartment, she had no idea even existed on the station.

But now the break was over, and they had been apart for three weeks already. This hadn't been hard last year. Keeping in touch by sending messages back and forth had been kind of fun and exciting last year.

But this year? This year she missed being with him, and the messages just made her miss him more.

"Hey," Moreau said. Ritchie was afraid she had let her feelings show on her face and reached up to make sure she hadn't let a tear slip, but Moreau wasn't even looking at her. She was on her feet, reaching for her bag. "We're landing. Didn't you notice? What are you staring at out that window, anyway?"

"Nothing," Ritchie said, and forced a smile so she wouldn't have to say more.

The hovering train pulled up to a station platform set high atop a marble structure. When they stepped out of the train cars, they found themselves on an open-air platform, and the smell of the planet washed over Ritchie so intensely she instantly forgot anything else.

It smelled green. That was her first somewhat inarticulate impression. Then she started to pick the aromas apart. Flowers were the strongest scent, almost overwhelming all the others. But then she smelled ripe fruit and freshly mown grass. There was even a hint of something she was sure was honey.

And the sun on her face was so deliciously warm it made her skin tingle. There was a constant breeze, but it was a movement of warm air that stirred her hair but didn't take away any of that solar warmth.

"I can like this," she said, her eyes closed as she turned her face more directly towards the massive yellow sun.

"I wonder if there's a way to test out of our last year at Oymyakon and just move here right away," Moreau said wistfully.

"I thought you'd been here before?" Ritchie said, turning away from the sun to look at Moreau.

"Sure, for parties," Moreau said. "I kind of forgot how always perfect the weather is here."

"Cadets, follow me!" they heard the voice of Colonel Hansen calling from the far end of the platform. The two of them hoisted their bags up on their shoulders and followed the others as they marched down the endless back-and-forth stairway to ground level.

Ritchie recognized the building they were in as a transportation terminal. The platform for the intergalactic railway was very far from the main hub, and they walked past terminal after terminal servicing the far more common shuttle traffic. Although it was no where near as massive as the transportation hubs in space, she saw all the things she expected to in such a location: ticketing agents and food vendors and lots of weary, impatient travelers milling about.

But the building itself was like standing in a living museum. The marble looked so cool in contrast to the warmth of the air, and tendrils of greenery grew up the columns to knit across the ceiling high over-head, forming something like a forest canopy. She could hear birds singing and see them darting about. But technically, they were still indoors.

"Is everything here like this?" Ritchie asked, as Moreau had to come back a third time to fetch Ritchie and hurry her to follow the others. Everything kept catching her attention. This time it was a perfectly ripe golden pear hanging just over her head, so close she could reach out and touch it.

"Everything is like this," Moreau said. Then she reached up to pick the pear. She had to hop a little, short as she was, but she caught it, took a deep breath of its sweet aroma, then handed it to Ritchie.

"We can take it?" Ritchie asked, looking around to see if anyone was about to come running to chastise them.

"You can pick anything. It just grows back," Moreau said. "Eat it."

Ritchie took her own deep inhalation of the pear's smell. Then she bit into flesh still warm from the sun. The skin burst against her teeth and sticky juice filled her mouth.

It was perfection.

"Come on. We have to catch up with the others," Moreau said to her, and Ritchie nodded but kept eating the pear as they walked through a maze of hedges, following cobblestone paths that split, diverged, and rejoined in the sort of knot work patterns she had seen from the train above.

It would be very easy to get lost here. Especially the way sound travelled through all that greenery. It always sounded like they were about to come upon a large group of laughing and chatting cadets, but every corner they rounded they were still alone.

"You know where we're going?" Ritchie asked Moreau. She had finished her pear and now looked at the core, unsure what she should do with it. It was too sticky to put in her pocket.

"Your implant will guide you if you need it," Moreau said. "But it's not as complicated as it looks. The patterns repeat a lot. You'll get the feel for it." Then she took the core from Ritchie and tossed it under a hedge as they turned the next corner. "Compost," she said at Ritchie's horrified look.

"Implant, right," Ritchie said. Once upon a time, Ritchie had used her implant for everything. She had trusted it implicitly.

But the events of the last few years had destroyed that trust. She had turned off all the things that used to run automatically, so she had to give a mental command to bring up her own guidance system. Now, at every branching point, the correct path to take her to their assigned dormitory lit up in her vision ever so subtly.

They took a few more turns through the hedge maze, then emerged at the back of an open lawn. The grass here had been mown in an overlapping pattern of diamonds, and the smell of the cut grass was still fresh in the air. The other cadets were already across the lawn, gathering on a patio that jutted out of the back of a three-story marble building topped with domes of the same creamy stone.

The two of them jogged across the freshly mown grass to reach the others before their tardiness was noticed.

"Cadets, you already have your room assignments," Colonel Hansen was saying as they climbed the three steps to the patio level. "You have a bit of time to find your beds and unpack, but you must be back down here to this patio for your orientation tour. Don't be late!"

Ritchie consulted her implant and found the memo with her room and bed assignment, but before she could ask Moreau if she had gotten hers, she got another message. She had a brief moment's hope that it was from Guy, but that died at once. It was Hansen, asking her to wait on the patio after he dismissed the other cadets.

"I'm supposed to stay here," Ritchie said to Moreau.

"Me too," Moreau said.

"Is this a task force thing?" Ritchie whispered. Only then did she remember that while they had left Kristof Wyss and Tassa Sokolov behind at Oymyakon with the other cadets in the lower three classes, Fitz was meant to be with them on this field trip.

She hadn't seen him on the train, but that hadn't been unusual. Once upon a time, they had been best friends. But that had been as little kids. They had started out as close friends again when they had met as cadets, but that hadn't lasted.

Not that she had any idea why. Something had just... changed.

Nowadays, he avoided her a lot, and she had trained herself to stop feeling hurt by that. Well, the training was an ongoing affair, but it was successful in the sense that she didn't always notice when he wasn't there. His absence had become part of her mental *familiar* column.

"Where's Fitz?" she asked, looking around.

Moreau sighed what was to Ritchie's ears an overly dramatic sigh. But then she pointed to the far end of the patio, closest to the back wall of the dormitory building itself, in the shadows from the afternoon sun.

There he was, standing alone, hands in his pockets and his head down as if half-napping. Maybe it was because he was in that gray shadow and not in the bright sun with the other cadets, but he looked pale to her eyes. Too thin, too tired.

But his dark hair was as thick as ever. Especially that one particular lock that always fell over his forehead, even when he wasn't tipping his head down, as he was just now like he was trying to accentuate it.

Her fingers itched to brush it back, but that wouldn't go down well. He barely tolerated her talking to him these days.

Still, he looked like he needed a friend. What could've happened to make him look so forlorn?

"What's wrong with him?" Ritchie asked Moreau. Because as much as he had closed himself off to her, he did still sometimes talk with the others.

"I wouldn't call Shackleton Fitz IV being antisocial 'wrong'," Moreau said. "Not in the sense of being unusual."

"Still. Is something going on I should know about?"

Moreau sighed again, but didn't follow it up with anything for a really long time.

"Moreau," Ritchie said at last.

"If I had to guess, I would say it's because the Berwegers are here," Moreau said. "Or did you forget?"

"No, I didn't forget," Ritchie said, although that was only half true. She had known they would be here. They were both first years at the diplomat school. She had been preparing herself for the inevitable encounter with them as much as she could.

But it was almost impossible to prepare to face someone whose uncanny charisma and illegal pheromone enhancements could put anyone in a sort of mindless thrall.

And it was worse when both twins were acting together.

"Shouldn't Fitz look happier if he's about to be reunited with Feena?"

"After a mere three weeks?" Moreau countered. Ritchie felt her cheeks heat, and Moreau actually looked embarrassed by her own words. "Also, technically, they broke up," she said.

"What was the story, though?" Ritchie asked. "Amicable mutual decision, I thought. Or that was the plan when Hansen told me."

"That was the plan," Moreau agreed. "And honestly, I don't know anymore than you do about what was really going on there."

"He was using her to get information about what her family is up to," Ritchie said with more confidence than she felt.

"That was the intent," Moreau said. "But either Fitz is a better actor than I ever suspected, or somewhere along the way, feelings got involved."

Ritchie glanced over at Fitz, who was among the few lingering at Hansen's command as the others wandered into the dormitory.

She really hoped that Moreau was wrong. She hoped Fitz was putting on a masterpiece of acting even now with all the gloomy moodiness.

Because the alternative was too horrifying to contemplate.

2

AFTER ONLY A SINGLE DAY, Shackleton Fitz IV already missed the miserable weather of Oymyakon. The constant storms of wind, rain and snow pelting down on the Foreign Service Academy, buildings and cadets both, so perfectly matched his mood over the past months, it felt wrong to be anywhere else.

It had felt wrong being with his mother in their townhouse on the capital world of Jorda. The warm, bright sun and plethora of cultural activities and especially his mother's entire glowing personality had jarred badly against his own miserableness. He had toyed with staying on Oymyakon over the break with the kids who couldn't afford a ticket home, but in the end had answered his mother's summons.

But not on account of her, really. He had hoped for a moment along with his father. But his father was at an undisclosed location, dealing with an undisclosed but crucial problem. It had been impossible even to send him a message, and so far as Fitz knew, it still was.

His consolation prize had been the near-constant presence of Feena Berweger, who had also spent the break on Jorda with her uncle and aunt. Fitz had let her drag him along to every ballet, opera, concert, and party she had a fancy to go to. Because being with her felt almost as appropriate to his mood as being on Oymyakon.

Infuriatingly, she never seemed to mind, or even notice.

Then school had resumed, but he only had a few weeks to bask in Oymyakon's miserable climate before being packed up with the other last-year cadets to visit Braga, the university planet.

He had been here before, many times, for parties in years gone by. He knew how perfectly wonderful the climate here was. The sun was warm; the breeze was a constant stirring that brought a melange of delicious smells without ever making you cold. Rain fell in the hours before dawn, almost as if Braga had a controlled weather system like some of the resort worlds had.

He was not enjoying the perfection. His only consolation was that somewhere among all these decadent gardens filled with gorgeous, scented flowers and ripe fruit begging to be tasted was Feena Berweger.

And her brother too. Finn hadn't been on Jorda, but he was definitely here on Braga. It was almost like Fitz could sense his presence. And like Finn in his turn sensed him as well. It was only a matter of time before their paths crossed.

"Hey, Fitz!" One of his roommates, Boone Stucki, called to him, snapping him out of the reverie that had left him standing beside his bed, looking down at his unzipped but not yet unpacked bag. "Time for the first tour, man. Shake a leg!"

"Which one comes first?" Fitz asked, leaving his bag as it was to head back down the stairs with Stucki.

"Guardian," Stucki said. Fitz was just noticing that Stucki's buddy Kye Imhof wasn't there with them when Stucki added, "are you doing both, then?"

"Yeah, that's why I was late getting up to the room. Those of us looking at both schools had some extra instructions," Fitz said. Although he didn't know why he was bothering looking at both now. He knew he was going to apply for guardian school. There was no question in his mind about that. Plus, the Berweger twins were both at the diplomat school. Skipping that tour was his best chance at avoiding them all together.

But he had signed up for both tours. Because he knew Ritchie was signing up for both tours.

"You all right?" Stucki asked, and Fitz realized he had just sighed his frustration out loud.

"Yeah, fine," Fitz said. "I think all this sunlight is giving me a headache."

"You're crazy," Stucki said, but somehow managed to say it fondly. Then he shook his head and laughed. "Man, I hope you pick guardian. I'm really going to miss you otherwise."

"Imhof isn't here. Does that mean he's already settled on diplomat school?" Fitz asked.

"Yeah. New buddy for me next year," he said.

"New buddies for lots of us," Fitz said, thinking of his own buddy. Kristof Wyss had been assigned to him even though he was a year behind Fitz. Which meant Wyss would go through his last year at Oymyakon either buddy-less or buddied up with some other unpartnered cadet.

Fitz starting out new in a new school would be assigned someone too, but after so many academies over so many years, he no longer cared who was assigned to him.

But he was going to miss Wyss. That went without saying.

They reached the patio to find the other cadets already moving down the steps, across the mown lawn to one of several openings in the hedge wall beyond. Fitz and Stucki fell into step at the back of the group.

Fitz could see Stucki drinking the whole environment in and realized he had no idea where Stucki was from. Had he grown up on a single isolated space station like Wyss and Ritchie for the last part of her childhood? Or was he from a wealthy family who travelled across the Union of Free Worlds at leisure, like Fitz himself or Ritchie's buddy Moreau?

Fitz was mildly curious, but not enough to ask. He just watched as Stucki paused mid-step to sniff at the heart of a blossom the size of a dinner plate. He curled up his nose and tried to fan the smell away.

"The big yellow ones are a bit noxious," Fitz warned him. Then, despite himself, he added, "the little white ones don't look like much, but they have the best scent. I don't know what they're called, but they smell better than the others."

"These?" Stucki said, grabbing a few that were growing in a cluster. Whatever plant they were, they blossomed off of parasitic vines that twined through the limbs of the hedges. Stucki inhaled deeply, then gave Fitz an emphatic nod. "You're right."

They emerged from the hedge maze onto another immaculate lawn. This one was even larger than the one that ran up to their dormitories, and it appeared to wrap around the entire squarish building of black-flecked marble. The voices that carried to them from parts unknown sounded like soldiers chanting in time. Someone somewhere was doing physical training.

"Welcome, cadets!" said a voice that sounded familiar. Fitz turned his attention to the two waiting guardian cadets at the top of the stairs that led up to the front entrance of the guardian school. He recognized both the cadets waiting there at once, although it was the young man who had spoken.

Dario Bale. Fitz would know those twists of black hair anywhere, as well as that wide grin. Bale had been cadet captain when Fitz had started at the Oymyakon Foreign Service Academy.

The young woman next to him, Nicol Egli, hadn't been cadet captain when Fitz started, but she had been appointed before the end of his first year to take the place of her buddy Hanne Jeger after Jeger had died in a tragic accident. Egli had cut her brown hair short since he had seen her last, but it was still as neatly arranged as ever.

"I see some familiar faces," Bale said as he smiled down at all of them. "I'm hoping to see you again next year. But first, let's get started with the tour. Any questions at any time, just grab me or Egli here."

Egli leaned over and whispered something in his ear, and he nodded.

"Right, and I'm Bale, for those of you who don't know me," he said. "Let's go!"

Bale and Egli led them all into the massive front hall of echoey marble walls and decorative columns. It all felt a bit much, the grandiosity, but once past that hall, things scaled down to normal-sized hallways that led into classrooms, training rooms, exercise rooms, barracks and a mess hall. It wasn't much different from back on Oymyakon.

It was nicer, but not fundamentally different.

"Hey, Fitz," Bale said, suddenly appearing at Fitz's elbow. Egli at the front of the group was directing them all to the cadet lounge and library, and for a moment the crowd parted to give Fitz a full-on view of Ritchie's face as she looked up at the engraving of the school logo over the doorway to the auditorium.

She was enthralled. Of course she was.

"Hey, Bale. Good to see you," Fitz said. He tried to summon up more enthusiasm, but even on his best day, he couldn't match what Bale brought, and this was far from his best day.

"I wanted to be sure to talk to you personally," Bale said. "Do you mind if we peel off for a bit? I can show you the lounges and stuff after."

"Yeah, no problem," Fitz said, and let Bale lead him down a narrow corridor to a tiny office. It was long and narrow, and the two desks it contained were staggered so that anyone trying to cross to the far wall would have to serpentine around them. Bale slipped past the first one, pausing to grab the chair and spin it around to face the second desk.

"What do you think?" Bale asked as he shimmied around the second desk to sit down in that chair. Fitz sat down across from him and looked around.

"It's nice. Airy, so it doesn't feel cramped. Smells like Braga everywhere, doesn't it?"

In truth, as much as he could smell the flowers and fruits from the gardens, the strongest smell in this particular room was a chemical lemon smell he assumed was some sort of cleaner. But he opted not to mention it.

"Is this your office?" he asked instead.

"Maybe someday," Bale said with a grin. "I'm only a second-year. This is the cadet captains' office. But they're letting me borrow it."

"Because?"

"I wanted to talk to you about your school choice," Bale said. "You're down as undecided. Can that possibly be right?"

"At the moment," Fitz said evasively. "Why?"

"Come on! You totally belong here. Don't you feel it?" Bale asked.

He held up his hands as if inviting Fitz to soak up some feeling coming from the school itself.

"It looks great," Fitz said. "Of course I haven't seen the diplomat school yet."

"That's a great school. I won't say otherwise," Bale said. Now he was the one sounding evasive.

"But?"

"Well, you tell me after you see it, but I just find the whole place so cold every time I visit it," Bale said, shivering as if from the memory.

"Everything is warm on Braga," Fitz said.

"No, the temperature is fine. I'm talking about the people, I guess. They're so cold," he said.

"Diplomats study emotional control, or so I've heard," Fitz allowed.

"Yeah, but even so. There's no camaraderie there. Not like here," Bale said.

"Do you think that's something I'm looking for?" Fitz asked, genuinely amused. Didn't Bale remember him at all? Fitz was a loner, and he had cultivated a reputation as one on purpose.

"I think you should," Bale said, unbothered by Fitz's attitude.

"I don't know," Fitz said, but Bale pressed on.

"Haven't you seen the way the other cadets are watching you?" Bale asked.

"The other Oymyakon cadets?" Fitz asked, confused.

"No, the guardian cadets. When we pass the classrooms or training rooms. Come on, I know you've seen them looking your way."

Bale leaned across the desk, eyebrows raised. Fitz cast his mind back to everything he had been tuning out while sleepwalking through the tour.

He came up with nothing.

"Weren't people just looking at us because we're a tour group passing through?" Fitz asked.

"No, this time of year we get them constantly," Bale said. "Well, maybe I should've waited until after the party to talk to you."

"There's going to be a party?" Fitz asked, even more miserably than before.

"It's pretty much starting now. If you don't mind skipping the rest of the tour, let's head there now," Bale said.

"Whatever," Fitz said resignedly. He guessed he didn't need to have Feena clinging to his arm for a party to feel like penance. Lately, he hated having people around him, no matter who they were.

Bale led the way back to the main corridor and then through the long stacks of the library to the back door. Beyond was another wide patio, this one still in full sun, although that sun would be setting shortly. Past the patio was another lawn, but its immaculate diamond pattern was marred by the random arrangement of cocktail tables dotting all over it.

Most of the other Oymyakon cadets were already there. Fitz's eyes found Ritchie at once, chatting with Moreau and Egli. She looked terribly interested in whatever Egli was saying to her.

"Just a little meet and greet with whoever isn't in class at the moment," Bale said, misreading Fitz's sudden hesitation. "But in this case, there are going to be more than a few cadets who are skipping class to make that party. And it's just to see you."

"Come on," Fitz said, irritated at being given the hard sell.

"Well, you and Ritchie," Bale amended. "You must know you're famous here."

"Famous for what?" Fitz asked.

Now Bale was the one who looked confused. "For what? For solving how many crimes now?"

"A few," Fitz admitted.

"And how many conspiracies have you exposed?" Bale asked.

"Still working on the first one, actually," Fitz said. But the words came out without his mind really being on them. He and Bale were still standing on the sun-warm marble of the patio, looking down at the rest of the party. Now that Bale had brought it up, he realized that people *were* looking his way more than was usual. And even more people were looking at Ritchie.

Ritchie, who didn't seem to notice at all.

"I think I approached this all wrong, didn't I?" Bale asked.

"What do you mean?" Fitz asked.

"You hate being famous," Bale said.

"I would if I thought I was," Fitz said. "You think I'd want to go here rather than the diplomat school because I have, what, fans here?"

"No. It's going to be the same at the diplomat school on that level," Bale said. Fitz felt his stomach sink. "But what I really meant to say was that you and Ritchie, you solve crimes."

"When we have to," Fitz said.

"All right, but there's not really a diplomat path that leads to crime solving," Bale said. "But one of the tracks past this guardian school is the crime investigation program. Which was why I was so surprised to see both you and Ritchie on the undecided list. Don't you want to continue your career of solving crimes?"

"I don't think either of us ever considered this an actual career," Fitz admitted, but he realized how that sounded to Bale's ears. Completely unbelievable.

But he really hadn't. All he had ever wanted with his life's journey was to spend it with Ritchie.

And so far, that wasn't working out at all.

"You've really not looked into the post-guardian programs at all?" Bale asked.

"Did you before you got this far?" Fitz countered.

Bale laughed. "Fair enough. That's why you're all here. Just promise me you won't commit to the diplomat school without giving me a chance to fill you in on what the guardian school has to offer."

"Aren't there more guardians than diplomats in the first place?" Fitz asked.

"True, but we always need more," Bale said. "All right, enough shop talk. I don't want to keep you from the party. I think I saw Ritchie just over there with Egli and Zahnd."

"I know where she is," Fitz said.

Then he walked down the patio steps to the lawn and headed to the farthest point from where Ritchie was standing, deep in conversation with an entire knot of guardian cadets.

3

FOR RITCHIE, everything was happening too fast.

She wished they could've been given more than a fraction of an hour to settle in after arriving at the dormitories. She had barely had time to unpack after Hansen's speech to the undecideds, let alone explore the world of Braga that was everywhere beckoning to her.

To wander aimlessly through the kilometers of hedge mazes, to follow every scent to its original fruit or flower, to just bask in the warmth and the deliciousness of the ever-present soft breeze. Why couldn't they have gotten a day or even just an afternoon to adjust a little?

But they had been hustled off to a whirlwind tour of the guardian school, whipping through room after room with barely a moment to soak any of it in. She had seen classrooms with interesting bits displayed on the screens, but had no time to take a better look. They had been whisked through the library too quickly to glimpse any of its offerings. There hadn't even been time to see what was on the menu when they jogged through the cafeteria.

And now they were at a party that didn't feel relaxed at all. It was like she was on some sort of audition, but she didn't know for whom or what she was supposed to perform.

At least the drink they had given her was good. Some sort of cool, creamy, spicy tea with more caffeine than she usually had so late in the day, but at the moment that jolt was just what she needed.

"What do you think?" Moreau asked as she sipped at her own tea.

"About the school?"

"Or whatever," Moreau said with a shrug.

"I don't know. I really don't. I wish we could see some classes in session or something. How are we supposed to decide just based on a tour of the building?" she asked.

"Oh, don't worry. This is just day one. Leaving your head reeling is totally part of it," Nicol Egli said as she approached the cocktail table where Ritchie and Moreau were standing together. Another cadet, also in full uniform, was walking beside her, but she had no glass in her hand. Most of the other guardian cadets on the lawn with the Oymyakon cadets were dressed for class, varying by whether they had been in physical training or classroom lectures or tactical drills, so this woman, being in a formal uniform, stood out a little bit. But even without that difference, she would be memorable. Her blonde hair was cut in a short, above the ears style that a lot of cadets were wearing, but her dark blue eyes were striking.

"So we *do* get to observe the classes at some point?" Ritchie asked, relieved.

But that relief died pretty quickly when Egli gave her a mischievous grin as she said, "observe? You'll be participating. And I promise you, no one is going to cut you any slack for still being an academy cadet. You'll be working physical training as hard as the rest of us, and you'll be called on in lectures and expected to give answers the same as the rest of us."

"It's just to be sure you're mentally prepared for your first year here," the other cadet said. "It's tough, that first year. A lot of washouts. It's best to know it's coming."

Ritchie's growing apprehension must have been showing on her face, because Egli quickly added, "it gets better. The first semester is absolutely the worst, but it gets better after that."

"The classes don't get easier," the other cadet said. "The cadets get better."

Egli thought this over, head tipped to one side. Then she nodded. "True," she said, and took a sip of her tea.

"I'm sorry, we haven't been introduced," Ritchie said, putting out a hand to the blonde cadet. "I'm—"

"Murdina Ritchie," the cadet finished for her with a smile, then gave her hand a warm shake. "I know. I pestered Egli into letting me meet you. I'm Pascale Zahnd. I'm a huge fan of your work."

"My… work?" Ritchie repeated numbly.

"In crime investigation. That's my primary guardian specialty too," Zahnd said.

"Oh. I…" but Ritchie trailed off, unable to collect her thoughts.

"Zahnd, I've already told you that Ritchie here is still undeclared," Egli said. "She's visiting the diplomat school next."

"Really?" Zahnd said with unfeigned surprise. "I know there's a backdoor way for diplomats to get into crime investigation through the psychology and profiling side, but I just assumed you were taking the direct path."

"I honestly haven't even thought that far down the road," Ritchie admitted. "I have to choose the guardian or diplomat track first before I can even think about the specialty I'll pursue in four years."

"I assumed you had a calling," Zahnd said, her cheeks flushing a little in embarrassment.

"It's just, my father was a diplomat," Ritchie said, not quite choking on the words. She avoided talking about her father with her friends. She hated doing it with strangers. "I don't think I want to follow his path, but I want to stay open to the possibility. I haven't even seen the school yet."

"So if we're undecided, we do these participation days with both schools?" Moreau asked.

"Yes. You split your time," Egli told her. "But I should warn you, both schools will be pulling out all the stops. Full-on high-pressure sales."

"For everyone?" Moreau asked.

"Well, for you two, for sure," Egli said. "And your friend Fitz, too."

"Because of what you've already done," Zahnd said, and her enthusiasm started bubbling over again. "Honestly, it was such a hassle switching shifts so I could be here today, but I really wanted to meet you. I'm already interning part-time with the crime investigation unit, you know. I help out with the bureaucracy mostly, but I get to do a few ride-alongs. Nothing so interesting as what you've done, for sure. On Braga, almost every crime is a party-gone-out-of-control sort of thing. But I'm in my last year here at the guardian school, which means when you start I'll be gone already. I know this party isn't the place, but I'd love to set up a time to meet with you and go over some of the cases you've worked. I have *so* many questions."

"I don't know what answers I could possibly have," Ritchie said. "Honestly. I didn't go looking for any of the crimes I investigated. I just happened to be there."

"Lots of people happened to be there," Zahnd said with a dismissive wave. "A train full of people. An academy full of people. But each time, you were the one who felt compelled to dig until you had the answers."

"I think Zahnd might be right," Moreau said. The corners of her mouth were doing that little wrinkling thing that only from long experience did Ritchie know meant she was drily amused. "I think you *do* have a calling."

"I don't know what work I want to do yet. I really don't," Ritchie said, suddenly feeling twice as overwhelmed as she had just a few minutes before.

"There's no rush," Egli assured her.

"It's like at the academy, you don't really have to start thinking about what comes next until the beginning of your final year. For now, just focus on picking us over the diplomat school," Zahnd said.

"Way to be impartial," Egli said, rolling her eyes.

"I have to get back to the office," Zahnd said with a sigh. "I'm going to ping you my contact info. Please let me know when we can meet for coffee or something and chat for an hour or so."

"I will," Ritchie said.

"Later in the week," Zahnd added. "I know there is a lot to take in the first few days, but by the end of the week, you'll feel calmer. Ping me then."

"I will," Ritchie said, with more confidence this time.

Then she and Moreau were alone with their teas again.

"Have *you* thought about what your primary speciality is going to be?" Ritchie asked Moreau.

"Are you kidding? I'm on the undecided between the two main branches list the same as you," Moreau said.

"Yeah. So is Fitz," Ritchie said, and found herself scanning the crowd for a glimpse of him. He always seemed to be so far away from her.

But never quite out of sight. She spotted him on the shadowy edges of the lawn by the first row of hedges. He was standing with Stucki and a few of the guardian cadets.

"Fitz is just waiting for you to make a choice," Moreau said.

"What, so he can pick the other thing?" Ritchie said dismissively. Then she thought it over and worried she was right.

"I don't know," Moreau said, as if her own answer surprised her. "Maybe. I just know he's definitely waiting for you to make the first move."

"Well, I can't make my decision based on what he might do," Ritchie said.

"No, I wouldn't recommend that," Moreau agreed. She swirled the last of the tea at the bottom of her glass to pick up some of the grains of spice that had clung to the sides. "But tell me the truth. Are you really undecided?"

"You don't think I am?" Ritchie asked.

"I think you want to give both branches a chance for the sake of your father's... memory is probably the wrong word," Moreau ended in a low mumble.

"No, I get what you mean, though," Ritchie said. She felt the old familiar stab at her heart that always gripped her when anyone implied that her father was dead and not just missing. But Moreau knew how she felt about that. She wasn't being insensitive. It was just a hard concept to work into a conversation without derailing it.

"You've been clear in the past that you don't want to do diplomat work," Moreau pressed.

"I don't want to do what my father did," Ritchie agreed.

"Even though by all accounts you excel at it," Moreau said.

"Whose accounts?" Ritchie demanded.

"Um," Moreau said, and to Ritchie's shock, her buddy's cheeks actually started to color. Moreau never got *this* embarrassed. What was this?

"Moreau?"

"Wyss has shown me some things," she said evasively. "Don't be mad."

"Like what?"

"Like your academic assessments. And some older things," Moreau said, not meeting her eyes. "They were almost universally good, you know."

"Like that matters. Why were you and Wyss digging into me?" Ritchie asked.

"We dug through all of Fitz's records too," Moreau said. "And Wyss knows everything about me. Probably more than I know about my own record, actually."

"Again, why?"

"It seemed important at the time," Moreau said. "As much as I think crime investigation might be a calling for you, there's no arguing that crime just keeps happening around you. It's good to have that baseline work done on all of us to have it ahead of time in case any of us ever looks guilty of anything."

"Does Fitz know you did this?" Ritchie asked.

"No, it was just me and Wyss," Moreau said, draining the last of her tea. Then she added, "and Sokolov."

"Sokolov too? What a conspiracy," Ritchie scoffed. Then another thought struck her. "Does Hansen know? Is he in on it?"

"No and no," Moreau promised her. "The point I was making is that from where I'm standing, you really have two callings. A guardian with a primary speciality in crime investigation, or a diplomat with a primary speciality in first contact communications."

"And I absolutely don't want to do the latter," Ritchie said. "But there are a wealth of options I haven't tried yet."

"You think you might have more than two callings?" Moreau asked.

"I might be good at more than two jobs, yes," Ritchie said. "I mean, given the proper training, I could be good at lots of things."

"Of course," Moreau said.

"There are a lot of things to do after diplomat school that don't involve first contact communication," Ritchie said. "Some of them just might be my thing."

"Sure," Moreau said with a shrug. "But if you want my opinion, you belong here in the guardian school. It's like you're already part of this world, just standing here at a party. Imagine you in classes," she said with mock enthusiasm.

"I don't have to. I'll be doing it later this week," Ritchie said, giving her buddy a playful shove. "But what about you? What's your calling?"

"Nothing calls me," Moreau said with another shrug. "I got into the academy for the worst of all possible reasons: to annoy my mother. I'm not sure that is going to be any use guiding my path here. I think, unlike you, I really am undecided at this point."

"Huh," Ritchie said, struck by another unexpected thought. "You know, I always assumed whatever came next, we'd still be together."

"You thought whatever you picked, I would follow?" Moreau asked, amused again.

"I know how it sounds," Ritchie said. "I'm sorry, I just didn't think about it at all. I just assumed. What if we pick different schools?"

"Look," Moreau said, taking Ritchie by the shoulders and turning her to face more or less due north. She pointed over Ritchie's shoulders to a dome of pinkish marble glowing in the rays of the afternoon sun. It was some distance away, just barely visible over the greenery, but Ritchie could make out the logo of the diplomatic corps on the white flag fluttering from a pole atop that dome. "That's the diplomat school. It's a few minutes' walk away. So what if we end up in different schools? We'll still be on the same planet. We'll still be friends."

"We'll always be friends," Ritchie said, as much to assure herself as Moreau.

"And your boyfriend might be on the far side of this world, but that's still only a few minutes away in his shuttle," Moreau said. "He might even be crashing this party right now."

"Not this party," Ritchie said with a sigh. "He promised to see me at the end of the week when my schedule is less chaotic."

"I don't know. Your end of week schedule is filling up pretty fast," Moreau said, raising an eyebrow.

"It will be easier seeing Guy next year, right?" Ritchie sighed.

"Not according to what these cadets are saying," Moreau said with a laugh. "Come on, let's get another glass of tea and try out some of those little cookies I keep seeing people munch on. This is a party."

"Cookies?" Ritchie said. She hadn't seen anything of the sort, but her stomach grumbled just at the word.

Making life-altering choices was hungry work.

4

FITZ HAD EXPECTED the diplomat school building to be a clone of the guardian school building, maybe with different decorations. But everything about the place had an entirely different vibe.

Every single room, whether classroom or cafeteria or dormitory, had an indoors/outdoors flow with part of the space being a paved garden area and part being an open-air room with plants growing everywhere.

Cool breezes blew down every hallway, and the warmth of the sun was always just half a step out from under this awning or that greenery-festooned trellis.

There was no one central entrance hallway, but large domed atriums marked key points throughout the school. Larger trees grew pillar-like under those domes, their branches entwining overhead. Those tree limbs muffled the sounds of cadets passing beneath them, but the domes over the limbs echoed those muffles.

It was a strange, almost unnerving acoustic effect. Like he was surrounded by whispers he couldn't quite make out.

Fitz knew that Braga had no real seasons, just the same mild climate year-round. So there was no hot, humid time of year where having chilling breezes blowing down every corridor would be appreciated. He had no idea why it was such a design feature. But it was probably why all the diplomat cadets, whose base uniform was the same as the guardians' but in different colors, all wore scarves or sweaters or shawls over their tunics. Many also wore hoods, although that might be because they found the constantly echoing yet inaudible whispers to be as maddening as he did.

Five minutes into the tour of the building, Fitz knew he was right to abandon his half-hearted plan to become a diplomat if Ritchie did what he thought she was going to do and became a guardian. There was just no way he could survive four years here.

Especially since somewhere lurking in these creepy halls were the Berweger twins.

Roughly a third of all foreign service academy cadets chose to be diplomats over guardians, but Fitz wasn't sure how that could be true. He didn't personally know of any besides the Berwegers. The two former Oymyakon cadets who were serving as their tour guides were both strangers to him, although they would've been last-years when he and Ritchie started.

And he was sure he would have remembered them if he had known them. They were both distinctive, even in uniform. Amelie Dauss was unusually tall and willowy thin, dark-skinned with her hair cut close to her scalp in a way that somehow made her seem even taller. The other cadet, Josif Bichsel, was more average in size, his brown skin a little more ordinary in hue, and he wore his hair in tight black knots much like Bale did, but he had a voice like warm honey and a way of moving that put Fitz in mind of his dancer mother. Every motion was deliberate and seemed to be speaking in some formal language Fitz couldn't quite decode.

But as fascinating as the guides were, it was hard for Fitz to pay much attention to their spiel. Partly because their voices kept getting lost in the whispery background, but mostly because Fitz, having decided this place was not for him, had a hard time working up the interest to keep listening.

Then he felt a prickle dance up his spine and knew he was being watched. But this wasn't the too-intent glances of cadets who knew who he was, like he had felt at the guardian school party the day before. No, this prickle was too familiar, too specific.

He fell to the back of the pack of cadets, then stopped walking and turned to look back at the atrium they had just left.

Finn Berweger was there, leaning with his back against one of those tall pillar-like trees, arms crossed as if he'd been there for hours, although Fitz knew for a fact he hadn't been there just a second before.

The diplomat colors of ivory and white-gold really shouldn't flatter him the way they did the darker-skinned Dauss and Bichsel. They should leave his fair features looking washed-out, pale.

They did not. Rather, his fair skin glowed with a rosy hue, and the piping on his uniform just brought out the threads of gold highlights in his blond hair. Fitz knew the twins had been created in a lab to have the very best features, among other more nefarious enhancements, but it still didn't feel quite fair.

Then he tore his eyes off Finn to see his sister Feena standing near the opposite tree. She was even more lovely, because of course she was. He felt that even before the moment her pheromones hit him. There was always that jolt, and as much as he could dismiss it after feeling it, he always felt it first.

For her part, she lit up the moment their eyes met, and she rushed down the hall to throw her arms around him.

"Fitz! I knew you'd change your mind and pick our school!" she said, after finally letting him go.

"I haven't picked anything yet," Fitz said. "I should really get back to the tour."

"Of course!" Feena said. Then she looped her arm through his, clearly intending to walk the rest of the tour with him.

Fitz looked back down the hall, but Finn had disappeared as suddenly as he had appeared.

"Don't you have a class?" Fitz asked, already knowing the answer.

"I can miss one class," Feena said with a laugh, hugging his arm. "Come on. Let's catch up."

"I don't have time for that," Fitz said.

"With the group, silly!" she said, then tugged on his arm until he hurried his steps to match hers.

As much as he dreaded what his fellow Oymyakon cadets were going to make of this spectacle in their midst, he quickly realized they weren't the only ones who had feelings about the two of them.

Given the open-air feel of all the classrooms, everyone passing in the corridor was in full view of the cadets sitting at desks. He could feel far too many pairs of eyes on him as he and Feena swept by. Some were curious or amused. But more than once, he felt something a lot closer to hostility.

"Are you sure we're going the right way?" Fitz asked as they turned down yet another corridor with no tour group in sight. How had he gotten so far behind so quickly?

"I know where they are headed," Feena assured him. "Do you think I'd ruin this for you? If you're still undecided, I want to do everything I can to get you to decide to come here, don't I?"

"I suppose you do," Fitz agreed.

"Isn't it gorgeous here? All the artwork comes from actual diplomatic missions, gifts from other cultures," Feena whispered to him. "I bet Dauss doesn't even mention that on the tour. I mean, look at that one. It was a gift from the yuffids. You know, before everything went so wrong."

"I *do* know," Fitz grumbled. It was irksome even from her, to be so dismissive of the species who had taken Ritchie's father from her. She knew full well it was best not to mention it in his presence. But he couldn't help looking in the direction Feena had pointed.

They were approaching a tall, ornate doorway, and across the top of the arch at the top of the doorway was a little shelf holding a strange sort of glass vessel. It didn't seem to have any practical use, but it was so stunning Fitz stumbled to a halt to look at it more closely. It was too high up to touch, but he gazed up at it.

The glass, if it was glass, had been blown into and through itself, an intricate tracing of delicate necks leading out of and back into the central heart-shaped chamber. And even as he looked up at it, he saw a small glittering cloud passing through one of those necks, turning and winding back to the chamber to hover there for a moment before moving down a different glass branch.

Fitz felt a shiver run up his spine. That something so beautiful could've come from the same people who had turned so violent without warning was hard for him to process. "Did Ritchie see this?"

"I doubt it," Feena said. Fitz could tell she was annoyed at the question, but he didn't care.

"She must've seen this," Fitz said. As disturbed as he was by looking at this object, how much worse would it be for her?

"Fitz, if she had seen it, she'd still be here," Feena said.

"You're right," Fitz said.

"Of course, I'm right," Feena said, then pulled his arm to get him moving again.

Beyond the doorway was the library, a massive space filled with as many trees as books, or nearly so. Desks were set inside nooks inside the trunks themselves, the leaves shading the working cadets from the sun overhead.

The guardian school library had been empty of cadets when they had passed through it, but this place was filled with cadets studying either alone or in small groups.

And finally, Fitz saw a few familiar faces. Nika Heim, whom he had met just the year before, was too intent over the tablet she was working on to see him wave to her. But Leodegrance Kung, a former Oymyakon cadet he had spoken with on a number of occasions, did notice and return the gesture before bending his head back over his own tablet.

"First year is very intense," Feena told him.

"You look perfectly relaxed," he noted.

"Don't I always?" she smiled at him.

"We're still not with the tour," he told her.

"This was the last stop on the tour," she said. "Your fellow cadets are just past those trees, on the north lawn."

"Another party?" Fitz groaned.

"Another party," Feena said. "I know how you hate them. But you're such a good sport when they're forced on you. You're going to do great. And I'm here to introduce you to absolutely anyone."

"I don't know who I'd even want to meet," Fitz admitted.

"You're really not interested in our school at all?" Feena asked with a faux-pout.

"Probably not," he said. They stepped out past the last row of trees onto a wide patio that progressed in a series of ever-lower platforms to the level of the lawn several meters away. Cadets from Oymyakon were mixing with diplomat cadets everywhere. But the diplomats were serving a lot more finger food and a wider variety of beverages, most of them hot.

"Well, that's just fine," Feena said brightly as she led him to the nearest table. "The two schools are quite close. We'll still see each other all the time. In fact, the diplomat school is hosting a mock dinner this evening. I believe you're all invited to this one, whichever school you're favoring. We underclass cadets will be working as servers, but the upperclass diplomat cadets are hosting, practicing all the protocols for formal interspecies gatherings."

"Interspecies?" Fitz asked, interested despite himself.

"For practice, that's the guardians," she said. "Of course I don't think you're alien at all."

"Thanks," Fitz said. Feena motioned for him to sit across from her at the table, then bent over to pour out a steaming cup of whatever sort of beverage was in the decanter. Then she filled a plate with one of every kind of nibbly bit from the three-tiered tray at the center of the table and set it in front of him.

He could feel it already, that companionship that had no business being between them. He was meant to be using their relationship to spy on her. For her part, so was she. They both knew it.

It was unsettling how much being with her felt like being with a friend. Maybe because no one on the outside knew what it was like for the two of them on the inside of this... whatever was between them.

Fitz bit into some sort of cheesy vegetable tartlet, but he was getting that prickling feeling up his spine again.

Finn was there.

Fitz grabbed a napkin to deal with the dripping hot cheese, but at the same time, he scanned the tables around them. He didn't see Finn, but he did see Ritchie, sitting with Moreau and a few other cadets. Finn might be watching her, but he wasn't in her vicinity actively engaging with her.

Not that Fitz knew what he would do if that happened. He doubted

Ritchie would appreciate him intervening between the two of them. Again.

Then he noticed another diplomat cadet, a young man with thick curls of reddish-blond hair whose green eyes were shooting daggers at Fitz.

"You might not think I'm an alien, but that doesn't seem to be a universal feeling," Fitz said, and dared another bite of the hot tartlet.

"What's that?" Feena asked, delicately wiping her fingertips on her napkin. Not that he'd seen her eating anything. But that kind of pretending was probably part of diplomat training.

"That red-haired fellow just off your right elbow," Fitz said lowly, without pointing. "Why does he hate me with the intensity of a thousand suns?"

Feena leaned over to help herself to a square of pastry dusted in copious amounts of powdered sugar. As she set it on her own plate, her eyes darted surreptitiously to her right. "Oh, him? That's nobody. You don't need to worry about him."

"Surely he's somebody," Fitz said, but Feena was frowning. Not at him, but at something past him. He resisted the urge to turn in his seat to look. "What is it?"

"My brother needs me," she said with another little pout. "If he's interrupting you and me, it must be important, right? I better go see what he needs."

"By all means," Fitz said.

But the minute she left, it felt incredibly awkward, sitting alone at that table. He noticed the red-haired cadet was also alone at his table.

Well, the point of this little exercise was to mingle, right? And he really wanted to know what was with this guy.

Fitz picked up his cup and saucer and started to walk over to the other table. But the instant the cadet saw Fitz coming, he threw his napkin down in disgust and stormed away from the entire party.

Leaving Fitz standing there holding a cup and saucer, completely flabbergasted.

"Are you doing all right?" a throaty voice asked. The voice was feminine, but came from a point decided above his shoulder. He turned to look up at the diplomat cadet Dauss.

"I'm all right," Fitz assured her. "Is he?"

"He?" she repeated, looking around and just catching sight of the man disappearing back inside the library. "Oh, yes. I'm sure he's quite all right. Would you like to sit?"

"I was sitting just back there," Fitz said, looking back at his abandoned plate of food. He couldn't see either of the Berweger twins anywhere.

"I'll sit with you," she said, gently touching a hand to his shoulder to encourage him to go back to the table. Then she settled into Feena's chair, delicately setting Feena's abandoned cup, saucer and plate to one side and helping herself to fresh ones.

"So who was that guy?" Fitz asked, then bit into a stuffed mushroom so it would feel more like a conversation than an interrogation.

"That was Nils Kaufmann," she said as she poured her cup half-full from the decanter and sprinkled a bit of salt over the surface before stirring it with a tiny spoon.

"Who's Nils Kaufmann?" Fitz asked. She raised an eyebrow at him, and he added, "he looks familiar, but I can't quite place him." Which was a total lie. He was sure he had never seen that guy before in his life.

"Kaufmann is a last-year diplomat cadet, the same class as me. As much as Bichsel and I are cadet captains, he is the top of the class academically and by pretty much any other measure. I'm not surprised if you think you've met him before. He just has that kind of personality where everyone feels like he's an old friend. He's very popular. Warm, likable, friendly."

"Really?" Fitz said, trying to tone down his skepticism with partial success. "I was just sitting here with Feena Berweger, and I would swear from the looks he was sending my way, I was his mortal enemy."

"Nils?" she gasped. As contrived as her gesture was, hand to her heart, too perfectly done, Fitz wasn't fooled. She had been shocked enough to switch to first names.

She really believed what she said about Nils, the warm, likable, friendly, popular guy.

"Not his usual temperament, I take it?" Fitz said casually, then popped the last of the mushroom into his mouth.

"No," she said, but too slowly. She sighed. "I wouldn't have said so for the seven years I've known him. We went to foreign service academy together as well," she added confidentially. Then she sighed again. "But this semester…"

She trailed off without completing her thought, but Fitz was pretty sure she didn't have to. "Feena Berweger enters into this, I'm guessing."

"Is she a friend of yours?" Dauss asked. There was just a hint of anxiety in her voice. Her answer was going to be different whether he said yes or no.

Which was tricky. Most of the Union of Free Worlds who cared about such things assumed the two of them were an item. It certainly looked that way to everyone save the two of them.

And maybe not even to both of the two of them. He had to admit he was never quite sure just what was going on in Feena's mind. She acted like she enjoyed it, the idea that they were spies working on different sides, each trying to out-spy the other.

But sometimes there seemed like something else was going on too. Something deeper, more genuine.

More disturbing.

"She went to Oymyakon Foreign Service Academy for the last two years," was all that Fitz said in the end.

"Oh. Of course," Dauss said with a very diplomatic smile. "Well, as lovely as Kaufmann is as a human being, he's always been someone who was not looking for a relationship. He's very ambitious, very career-focused. You have to be, to be the top of the program here at this school. I've never seen him really notice another cadet before. But he's definitely been noticing Feena."

"If it's any comfort, she's probably putting the whammy on him on purpose," Fitz said.

"The whammy?" Dauss said with a politely confused smile.

"Pheromones," Fitz said. But he was feeling a chill again, this time in every bone in his body. Were the Berwegers roaming a school where no one knew what they were capable of? Like apex predators swimming through a school of clueless prey?

"Oh," Dauss said. She didn't dismiss the idea at once. Fitz could see her mulling it over. He could almost see her putting together a thousand little moments over the last few weeks, putting them into a new context. A touch of color flushed across her cheeks.

"It all makes sense now?" Fitz guessed.

"It might," she said. Diplomatically, of course. "I hate to leave you alone, but I'm really meant to be mingling throughout the party."

"It's all right. I'll find someone to chat with," he promised her. She smiled and left, and Fitz reloaded his plate with most of the rest of the three tiers of food.

Chatting he could do without, but the food was actually pretty good.

He wondered what would be served at the formal dinner that evening.

5

IT SHOULD'VE BEEN a lovely party. Sitting at tables somehow felt more intimate than mingling while standing had been at the guardian school. She and Moreau had sat together at one of the tables, but a rotating pair of diplomat cadets were always with them, making polite chitchat and refilling their cups and plates. The food was amazing, and the three-tier trays had heating elements built into them that kept everything at the perfect temperature.

She knew the diplomat cadets were just as curious about her as the guardian cadets had been, but they were much subtler about looking at her and whispering together.

Well, all save one of them. Finn Berweger never once took his eyes off her. He never came any closer or attempted to talk with her, but just the constant presence of his gaze was enough to put her on edge.

"Do you want to walk through the gardens?" Moreau asked her. Ritchie looked over her shoulder at the arched trellis that led into the hedge maze. The scents of an impossible number of flowers were carried to her by the cool breeze, and she longed to walk those cobblestone paths and smell every single blossom.

But it was getting chilly. The sun was nearly gone from the sky, and the breeze had a bit of a bite to it. Nothing like the winds of Oymyakon, but enough to make her uncomfortable.

"Why don't we wander through the school?" she suggested instead.

"Sounds good to me," Moreau said, and they got up from their table. Ritchie could feel Finn watching her the entire time, even past the point where the trees that flanked the library should block her from his view.

"The art is fascinating, isn't it?" Moreau said, pulling Ritchie's attention away from Finn.

"I could spend a day just examining it all, that's for sure," Ritchie agreed. "I wish there were plaques telling the origin of everything."

"I bet there's a file somewhere we can access with our implants," Moreau said, then yawned. "But I'm not up for a directory search. I just want to enjoy it in blissful ignorance."

"Me too," Ritchie admitted. And not just because she was avoiding using her implant.

They passed through the library and into an atrium, then picked a corridor at random and followed it. They stopped every couple of paces to admire another piece of sculpture or hanging tapestry or digital hologram that lined the walls.

"What do you think?" Moreau asked her some time later.

"I think it's meant to be a couple of people under a tree, isn't it?" Ritchie asked, squinting at the painting they were standing in front of.

"No, I mean, what do you think of the school?" Moreau asked.

Ritchie thought it over. Then she realized she was rubbing her upper arms. "It feels cold, doesn't it?"

"It does," Moreau agreed. "And I'm guessing you don't mean the temperature."

"No, although that too. But I meant, doesn't everyone in the school feel almost excessively reserved?"

"I think it's part of the training," Moreau said. "I think it's rather refreshing after all the shouting and running around we do at the foreign service academy."

"I think it's more than that, though," Ritchie said. "Something just feels wrong to me."

"Is it the Berweger effect?" Moreau asked.

"You think they whammied the whole school already?" Ritchie asked.

"Just you, and just now. You're on edge."

"No, it's not that. Haven't you noticed?" Ritchie said. Then she grabbed Moreau's arm, pulling her into an alcove off the atrium they were just passing through. She wanted to avoid the echo effect of the dome that only seemed to magnify more when what was spoken was in whispers.

"Noticed what?" Moreau asked.

"The cadets," Ritchie said. Then jutted her chin ever so slightly to point out a diplomat cadet on the far side of the atrium collapsed over a tablet. He had his head in his hands, pulling fistfuls of his hair as he focused on the tablet. It really looked like it must hurt.

"Studying?" Moreau asked.

"Just barely keeping it together," Ritchie said, then pulled Moreau after her to continue their walk. "Keep an eye out. Every private corner has a diplomat cadet in it who looks like they're about to have a total breakdown."

"First year is stressful," Moreau said. "That's what they all keep warning us."

"Yes, but here it's everyone," Ritchie said.

"I think you're imagining it," Moreau said.

Then they turned a corner and almost tripped over a cadet who was sitting against the wall with her legs sprawled out in front of her. She was even sagging to one side like a doll tossed roughly into a corner and abandoned. Her straight black hair hung loose around her, a frightening display of untidiness that would be out of place in either the diplomat or the guardian school.

And her blue eyes were red with unshed tears.

"Sorry!" she said, pulling her legs in and sitting up straighter. Then she scrubbed at her thin, almost hollow pale cheeks, as if drying away tears she hadn't actually shed.

"Are you okay?" Ritchie asked.

"Fine. Fine," she assured them. Then she at last gave them a proper look and saw their Oymyakon uniforms. "You're on a tour?"

"Just finished," Moreau said. "We wanted to take another look at the school rather than hang around at the party."

"Oh, dear," the cadet said with a nervous laugh. "Oh, please don't judge us harshly because of finding me like this. I'm really okay."

"You look a little burned out," Ritchie said.

"No, no," she said.

"Are you a first year?" Moreau asked. "They say it's the hardest, the first semester."

"No, I'm way past that," she said with an attempt at a smile. Then she got to her feet, brushed nonexistent dirt from her uniform, then held out a hand to them. "I'm Veronika Hefti, by the way."

"Antoinette Moreau," Moreau said, shaking Hefti's hand. "And this is Murdina Ritchie."

"Cadet Ritchie," Hefti said, as she shook her hand. Then she frowned, as if wondering why that name sounded familiar. But she just shook her head, as if dismissing the thought. "I'm a last-year student here. I actually have all my credits in. I could graduate now if I wanted to. Or I could just coast through the rest of the year."

"But?" Ritchie said.

Hefti gave them a somewhat more convincing smile. "I guess I'm just not built that way. I always have to push to be the best, you know? Not just that. There is so much still to be learned, and I want to learn it all. I can't waste any time. You know?"

"I think I do," Ritchie agreed.

The corner of Moreau's mouth twitched ever so slightly, but she said nothing.

"Honestly, this is a great school. Especially if you like research. Our library is so extensive, and there are so many options for open-study classes. You can design your own curriculum around your own inter-ests, like I have. We have so much more flexibility here than they do at the guardian school."

"What do you study?" Moreau asked her.

"Dining customs of different species," Hefti said. Then she blushed as she added, "specifically, the unspoken communication of place setting arrangement. Both who sits where but also how the utensils are arrayed at each place. I know, it's very niche."

"So you must be part of what's going on tonight, then?" Ritchie asked.

"All last-year cadets are. It's one of our big final assignments. The last year is full of things like this," Hefti said. "Next semester, we actually go to a non-union world to interact with a nonhuman species. I'm really looking forward to it. Of course it will be one of the safer, friendlier nonhuman species. Close allies of the Union of Free Worlds."

"That does sound amazing," Moreau said with something almost like enthusiasm in her voice.

"I'm sorry, but I really should get going. I was only going to stop here for a moment alone before heading into the library," Hefti said. Then she bit her lip and reached to grasp them both by the hand. "I know you wouldn't, because why would you? But will you promise me not to tell anyone you found me having a little moment? I swear it was nothing. And a lot of our grading here is by our peers. It's important no one knows I had a moment of weakness."

"Don't you all have them?" Ritchie asked, looking back over her shoulder at the other cadet still on the verge of tearing his hair out.

"Yes, but you don't get to be the best of the best by letting others see that side of yourself," she said with too forceful an attempt at cheer.

"We won't say a word," Moreau promised her.

"Thanks," she said and started to walk back to the library.

"Hair," Moreau said to her.

"What? Oh, right. Thanks!" Hefti said and gave Moreau one last smile before turning towards the library again. She finger-combed her hair as she walked, and by the time she turned the corner she had all of that long, sleek hair arranged in a braided bun at the nape of her neck.

"Well, I'm impressed," Ritchie said. "When my hair was long, I couldn't do that with two mirrors and a ton of pins, let alone while walking."

"I'll have to bring up my game," Moreau said, touching her own topknot. It was perfectly tidy, just as it always was, but it was a very simple arrangement compared to Hefti's braided knots.

"Aside from the hair, she reminds me of me," Ritchie admitted. "I don't know if I'd thrive in such an open environment."

"Come on. The only person I know who would love to design their own curriculum more than you is Wyss," Moreau said.

"That's the problem, though, isn't it?" Ritchie said. "I know just what Hefti means about wanting to learn absolutely everything. That could be me in four years, slumped on the hallway floor, completely burned out."

"I don't think your buddy would let you go that far," Moreau said. "But does this mean after the tour you're leaning more towards the diplomat school?"

"No," Ritchie said. "I think the guardian school is where I belong. But I haven't decided yet. I want to see what these classes are like first."

"You have a whole week before we have to decide," Moreau said. "Come on, let's head back to the party. Surely by now Finn Berweger has made himself scarce."

She nodded, but somehow, Ritchie doubted he was gone. But it didn't matter. In the end, there was no avoiding him.

If he wanted to get inside her head, he would find her wherever she hid.

6

THE SUN HAD SET, and the flowers had closed up for the night, but their scent lingered in the air as Fitz and the other Oymyakon cadets followed Colonel Hansen through the maze of gardens from their dormitory to the diplomat school. They were all dressed in their formal uniforms, which Fitz hated.

It wasn't that they were uncomfortable. They were designed to be moved around in the same as their daily wear. It was just that the earth tones of the Oymyakon Foreign Service Academy school colors were unappealing. Even against the greens of the gardens, they looked less like rich nutritive earth and more like a sickly sort of clayey mud.

Against the navy blues of the guardian uniforms and the cool ivory of the diplomats, they looked even worse.

But he'd be wearing navy blue soon enough, and for the rest of his career. He could get through one night in the worst shades of brown.

The sun had taken most of the heat with it when it had disappeared, and the ever-present breeze was almost chilly after the warmth of the day. But any worry Fitz had about being warm enough during the multiple courses of a formal dinner faded away when they crossed the last lawn to the wide patio decked out for the event. There were little heaters set everywhere, but especially around the tables. They gave off heat but only a soft red glow of light.

But the chandeliers free-floating over every elaborately laid table provided ample, sparkling light. And somewhere unseen, perhaps within the library itself, was a string group playing an unfamiliar song. It wasn't the sort of thing Fitz usually listened to, but it was the sort of thing that was easy to speak over while mingling before a meal, easy to tune out, but present enough to cover any awkward moments in conversations between strangers.

Fitz had eaten his fill at the last two parties, but when he smelled the sharp, herby cheese that was currently being served on trays by younger diplomat cadets, he decided he could eat a little more.

Just to be polite.

Colonel Hansen motioned for them all to huddle together on the grass before any of them could rush up the stairs to the patio and those trays of food.

"We are guests at this simulation," Colonel Hansen said. "This is a learning exercise for the diplomat cadets. The guardian cadets will be playing their roles as an alien species with specific predilections. They know what they are required to do. Your part is just to be what you are: human observers. Don't interfere with the lesson or be disruptive in any way, or you'll be answering to me. Understood? Fine. Then enjoy your dinner. You're free to make your own way back to the dormitories after the meal."

Fitz climbed the stairs and made a beeline to the nearest tray of cheese. He took a few squares and ate them one by one as he wandered through the tables, looking at the place settings. They were a bit more elaborate than he was used to, with a few unfamiliar utensils, but nothing he couldn't guess at the use for. But there were two glasses and two chairs for each plate. So that was weird.

There were also place cards with names written on them in a fine script. He checked his implant and found the message from the diplomat cadets with the seating chart so he could find his own table.

No one was sitting there yet when he arrived, but the other place card beside the single plate said, "Nils Kaufmann."

Well, he had wanted to have a conversation with Kaufmann. Not trapped together over the course of a long meal, but still. The opportunity to clear the air would be a good thing.

"I wanted to make sure you were in my section, but some upperclass cadet overruled me," Feena cooed as she swept up behind him to offer him a different appetizer: a small slice of toasted bread topped with a tomato and olive mixture.

"Probably for the best," Fitz said, as he took one of the toasts. "Have you seen who they put me with?"

Feena glanced down at the place card and made a face. But then she gave him a smile. "Honestly, I'm sure it will be fine. He's just a little obsessed with me, but I'm sure he'll be perfectly pleasant with you. Most people find him quite personable."

"So I've heard," Fitz said. "Please tell me I'm not in Finn's section?"

"No, he's serving the tables at the back," Feena said, pointing her chin towards the far end of the patio.

Fitz took a bite out of the toast thing and said, "and Ritchie?"

Feena narrowed her eyes at him briefly, then smiled again. "Far from both of us, of course. I know how you want things, Fitz."

"What's with the shared plates?" he asked.

"It's one of the customs of the species the guardians are pretending to be," Feena said, and her manner changed, like she was reciting something she had practiced more than a few times. "The guest chooses items from the serving trays, which will be presented one by one throughout the evening. Whatever the guest chooses, the host must take the first bite. Then the guest eats as much as they'd like. Whatever is left over, the host finishes."

"And I'm the guest?" Fitz guessed.

"Yes. So if you're feeling vindictive, you could leave your host with only a single bite of everything. Are you feeling vindictive, Fitz?" she asked teasingly.

He ignored the question. "It sounds like the species the guardians are pretending to be have a wariness of poison," he said.

Feena shrugged. "Most species do. But this one has a particularly long history of heads of state poisoning each other. So, yes, you're right."

"Well, at least I don't have to put my mouth on the same cup," Fitz said.

"You get your own cutlery as well," someone said behind him. He turned to see Kaufmann standing there in his diplomat cadet dress uniform. Fitz turned back again, but Feena had made herself scarce. She was already on the far side of the patio, offering her tray of toasts to a group of guardian cadets.

"I'm Fitz," Fitz said, thrusting a hand out.

"Shackleton Fitz IV," Kaufmann corrected him with a grin, but shook his hand.

"I don't usually say the whole thing," Fitz admitted. This was going better than he had feared. Whatever had made Kaufmann scowl at him so intensely before, it seemed to be a thing of the past now.

"I'm Nils Kaufmann," Kaufmann said.

Fitz nodded. "I've heard about you as well. All good."

"It usually is," Kaufmann said. Somehow, he didn't make that simple statement sound like the bragging it really was. "I believe they are about to get started. Shall we?"

"You're my host in this scenario?" Fitz asked, as they both sat down. "I would think you'd be at the head table. Isn't that the harder assignment?"

Kaufmann looked over at that table but wrinkled his nose. "This sort of thing isn't really my specialty."

"What is your specialty?" Fitz asked.

"Military strategy," Kaufmann said.

Fitz's mind flooded with dozens of followup questions, but they had to wait, as the diplomat cadet who had been assigned to serve their table brought the first of the trays over.

"You point out what you want, and I plate it up for us," Kaufmann told him. Fitz looked over the tray heaped with the roasted wings of some sort of poultry in an orangey sauce. Fitz pointed out a few pieces, and Kaufmann used the tongs from their place setting to move them from the tray to their plate.

"Are you supposed to take a bite from each wing?" Fitz asked. A single bite of each would be half the meat gone.

"I don't know. We don't have to stand on ceremony since it's just you and me at this table," Kaufmann said with a dismissive wave. "How about I take this one, and you can take that one? Just to start."

"Sounds like a plan," Fitz agreed, and they bit into the surprisingly spicy meat. Most formal dinners Fitz had been to growing up as the son of a general had featured the blandest food ever. This was a pleasant change. "So, military strategy? Isn't that more guardian territory?"

"It depends," Kaufmann said around a mouthful of food. He set the bone on the edge of his plate and wiped the sauce from his fingers before continuing. "Military strategy with the intent of replicating it is definitely guardian territory. But analyzing another culture's military history and strategy with the intent to understand it, and to advise leaders to be sure that they don't *misunderstand* it is definitely diplomat territory."

"Sounds like a lot of studying," Fitz said. Kaufmann nodded, but another server brought a tray down between them and Fitz was compelled to choose out which of three bowls of soup they should set on their plate.

"I'll just dip in once with a clean spoon and you can have the rest," Kaufmann said as he picked up his spoon.

"You're sure?" Fitz asked.

"I'm not particularly afraid of germs, but this sort of meal is definitely not my favorite," Kaufmann said, then slurped the soup from his spoon. He savored the taste on his tongue for a moment, then swallowed, giving Fitz a nod.

It was a potato and broccoli soup with more of that sharp, herby cheese making it almost too thick to call soup. If Fitz had known he'd be finishing it, he would've picked the clear broth one with the floating bits of green. But he was committed now. He didn't want to make Kaufmann finish what he couldn't eat.

As it turned out, everyone was right. Kaufmann was a very likable guy.

"My specialty is intensive, you're right about that," Kaufmann said as he nibbled at another wing. "But nowhere near as involved as yours."

"I don't have one," Fitz said.

Kaufmann laughed. "Come on. Everyone here knows who you are, and what you've done."

"I've noticed that," Fitz said. "It's weird."

"I admit I was excited when I saw the seating arrangement," Kaufmann admitted as Fitz looked over a tray of roasted fish and pointed out a couple of fillets for Kaufmann to move to their plate.

"Why?" Fitz asked, a sudden nervousness tightening in his chest. Was this conversation about to take a sudden turn towards Feena?

Fitz had never wanted less to talk about Feena.

"I was hoping after the dessert course you could introduce me to Murdina Ritchie," Kaufmann said, his cheeks flushing but not from the spicy sauce on the wings.

"Ritchie? I suppose that's possible," Fitz said, and put a forkful of roasted fish in his mouth. Although that would be decidedly awkward. When had he willingly spoken to Ritchie last? Had it even been this semester?

No, definitely not. She had gotten off the train practically aglow after her vacation with Guy Travert, and anything Fitz might have wanted to say to her had died unspoken.

"That would be fantastic. Really. I mean, I know you two do all your crime solving together, but there are things I would love to pick her brain about," Kaufmann said.

"So long as it's not about her father," Fitz said almost automatically.

Kaufmann had his mouth full of fish, but he nodded emphatically, as if he already understood that would be the case. He started to say something, but still had too much food in his mouth to open it yet, so he held up a single finger.

Fitz forced down another spoonful of the rich soup. Then he noticed the red blooms on Kaufmann's cheeks were spreading.

"It's okay. Lots of people are curious about that. Perfectly natural. It's just, I can't let you upset her like that. You understand," Fitz said.

Kaufmann was shaking his head now, and his face was redder than ever.

This wasn't a blush of embarrassment, though. Fitz was sure of that. He set his spoon down and put a hand on Kaufmann's back. "Are you all right?"

Kaufmann shook his head even more emphatically. Then he started to cough. At first, he tried to contain it. Apparently, his mouth was still full of masticated fish. But the cough built, and he quickly snatched up his napkin to cough into that over and over.

"Did you get a bone?" Fitz asked. He kept his voice calm, but inside he could feel a panic growing.

Something was very wrong here.

"Can you breathe?" Fitz asked, but he was already getting to his feet to stand behind Kaufmann. Kaufmann's coughing was more a wheezing now, as if he couldn't draw in breath to cough again but couldn't stop his body from trying to.

"Cadet Fitz?" Hansen called. He had been seated at the head table but was already halfway across the patio to where Fitz was already attempting to help Kaufmann clear any blockage. But even as he brought his fist up under Kaufmann's diaphragm, he wasn't sure he was doing the right thing.

What if his throat was closing up because of some sort of allergic reaction? Then why Fitz was doing wasn't going to help at all.

"He needs a medic!" Fitz yelled back to Hansen, but the other diplomat cadets were already converging on him en masse. One of them tried to pull him away from Kaufmann. Fitz slipped out of the grasping hands of the cadet, but stumbled forward into the table, shoving the plate. As thick as it was, the soup sloshed everywhere, and both of their drinking glasses were knocked over.

"Leave it!" Hansen said, grabbing Fitz by the arm and pulling him away from the table. "Step back. Let them work."

Fitz let Hansen drag him away, but he never took his eyes off of Kaufmann.

Kaufmann's face was no longer red. Now it was blue. What was going on?

Kaufmann looked up at Fitz and reached out a hand towards him. But he couldn't hold it up for more than a second. His arm fell back to his side and all the tension fell out of his body in a rush.

Fitz knew even before the medic arrived to say so that Kaufmann was dead.

He was also pretty sure it was a poison. He definitely hadn't been choking, and no allergy looked like what he had just seen. No, it had been poison. And poison meant it had been murder.

He looked at the plate of half-eaten food. All of it had been eaten by both of them in pretty much equal amounts.

How long until Fitz joined Kaufmann dead and blue on the floor?

7

RITCHIE WAS SHARING a plate with Diplomat Cadet Captain Dauss. This had clearly been arranged so that Dauss could put on the hard sell for Ritchie joining their school. But it wasn't as uncomfortable as Ritchie feared.

First of all, Dauss was meticulous in her duties as host, even to the point of waving certain servers over so they could sample the best dishes before the other tables, save of course the head table.

But on top of that, Dauss was just an excellent talker. Her voice was pleasant, and she was a first-class storyteller. All the details she remembered made whatever she was speaking about come to life.

Ritchie was just savoring a particularly tasty variation on coconut shrimp and seriously wondering whether the practical class in diplomacy that Dauss was currently describing wasn't really exactly what she hoped for in her post-academy experience, when a commotion on the far side of the patio caught her attention.

Or rather, it caught everyone's attention. Ritchie stood up as she saw Hansen jogging past her table. She followed him with her eyes and realized that Fitz was at the center of everything.

"Kaufmann!" Dauss gasped beside her.

Ritchie had to swallow the last of her shrimp, which was suddenly less captivating to her senses than it had been when she had put it in her mouth. Then she asked, "what's happening? Is this part of the experience? Because we weren't supposed to interfere."

But she knew even before Dauss shook her head that nothing happening now was planned. Not with the look of alarm she had seen on Hansen's scarred face as he had rushed by her.

"Fitz," Ritchie said, and started to move towards him. But Dauss caught her arm and held her still. "Let me go," Ritchie said, as reasonably as she could.

"Stay where you are," Dauss commanded her. "The authorities are already on their way. Everyone must stay where they are."

"But Fitz—" Ritchie said.

But Fitz didn't seem to be in danger. In fact, with his arms around Kaufmann's ribcage, it was clear he was trying to help Kaufmann get rid of whatever he was choking on.

Only it didn't seem to be working.

Diplomat cadets surrounded Fitz and Kaufmann, separating them. Fitz yanked his arm out of their grasp, knocking over everything on his table in the process. Then Hansen was pulling him back out of the way.

Ritchie could no longer see where Kaufmann was. He had fallen to the floor, and the table blocked her view. But she saw everyone standing around him gasp and a few turned away, already with tears in their eyes.

"He's dead," Dauss said in a wooden voice. Ritchie honestly wasn't sure if Dauss was talking to her or to herself.

"Lock down the scene," Guardian Cadet Captain Bale said, and all the guardians were instantly on their feet, making sure no one left the scene.

"What happened?" Ritchie asked. "Did he choke?"

"I don't think so," Moreau said, suddenly standing beside Ritchie. She had come from her assigned table some meters away and had brought a pair of diplomat cadets and a guardian cadet in her wake. The guardian cadet in particular looked annoyed that Moreau was ignoring him.

"Why not?" Ritchie asked, ignoring Moreau's tail as thoroughly as Moreau herself was. What difference did it make if they stayed at their respective tables or not?

"He turned some interesting colors," Moreau said grimly. "Plus Fitz was performing the maneuver correctly to clear his windpipe. No, it didn't look like choking. It might have been an allergic reaction."

"His throat closed up because of an allergic reaction," Ritchie said. She thought it through, then nodded. "Maybe."

"We are screened for all allergies when we start at this school," Dauss said. "Nothing served tonight is so exotic it wasn't covered in that screen."

Their conversation was interrupted by the sudden arrival of more guardians. But these weren't cadets, they were sworn officers of the crime investigation unit. Ritchie could tell by the patches on their uniforms and the styling of their hats.

An older woman with salt and pepper hair in a tidily short haircut and bright gray eyes raised a hand to get everyone's attention. Even Ritchie felt the alert ping to her implant commanding her to remain where she was and to be silent. The noise of dozens of panicked conversations died away, and only then did the woman speak.

"I am Chief Inspector Midja Kasteler, and I am in charge of this investigation. I understand this is alarming to you all and perhaps a bit of an inconvenience, but I do need you all to stay just as you are until we have the evidence locked down. My officers will be collecting statements from you. We will let you know when you are free to go, but for now, please remain seated at your respective tables until dismissed." She looked around the round, watching as several people sat back down at their tables. Although others like Ritchie and Moreau remained standing, she nodded anyway and said, "thank you."

"Should we sit?" Moreau asked.

"Yes, back at our table," the guardian cadet behind her said. Moreau rolled her eyes but didn't turn to face him.

Ritchie was about to suggest Moreau do as the guardian cadet clearly wanted. But when she saw one of the crime investigation officers shackling Fitz's wrists behind his back, all other thoughts flew from her mind.

"No," she said, and tried to make her way to Fitz, but she was stopped at once by several pairs of hands.

"You must leave it be," Dauss said to her in a gentle, motherly voice.

"You can't interfere," the guardian cadet said, even as he grabbed at Moreau's elbow to pull her back to where she was supposed to be.

"This is wrong. This is all wrong," Ritchie said, shaking off the hands that were still on her. Dauss's, but someone else's as well.

It was Pascale Zahnd.

"It's all right, Ritchie," said Zahnd. She wasn't in her dress uniform this time. Rather, she had the full patch and hat of the crime investigation unit, although her patch had a second strip underneath it that labeled her as an intern.

"They're arresting Fitz, but there's no way he's involved," Ritchie said.

"It's all right. It's just procedure," Zahnd assured her.

"Kaufmann choked or had an allergic reaction or something. Why are they arresting Fitz? How could that be procedure?" Ritchie demanded.

"Ritchie," Zahnd said gently. "As I'm sure you're aware, we have to rule out all possibilities. Until we know what happened, Fitz has to be confined. But I promise you, Chief Inspector Kasteler is very good at her job. She doesn't take any of this lightly."

"Remember who he is, Ritchie," Moreau said. "If anything is mishandled here, his father will be on this place with the full fury of his command. Fitz is going to be fine."

"Is he being accused of murder?" Ritchie demanded so forcefully that Zahnd actually flinched.

"I don't know. He's certainly a witness," Zahnd said.

"Who puts witnesses in handcuffs?" Ritchie asked.

"I don't know, Ritchie. I just promise you it's going to be all right. Please, just be patient." Then she turned to Moreau with a pleading look in her eyes. "I have to get to work."

"Of course," Moreau said, and moved closer to Ritchie as if taking charge of her. She tried steering a numb Ritchie back to her chair, but Ritchie regained her energy when she saw Hansen walking by, heading back to his own table. Ritchie pulled away from Moreau's grasp to run to the colonel and stand in his path.

"What's going on?" she demanded.

"Chief Inspector Kasteler is in charge," Hansen said. Ritchie glared up at him, irritated by that inadequate answer, and he looked ever so slightly contrite. "I don't know her except by reputation, but I assure you her record is good. She's not going to accuse Fitz of anything he hasn't done."

"Then why is he in handcuffs?" Ritchie demanded.

"At the moment? For interfering with a crime scene," he said. At Ritchie's blank look, he added, "he spilled food and drink all over the table. If this turns out to be a poisoning, he might have destroyed the evidence of it."

"That wasn't on purpose!" Ritchie said.

"I know, Ritchie. I was there," he said. "But I'm a guest here, same as you. I have no jurisdiction. I will do everything I can to look out for Fitz. Of course I will. But for now, I have to let the officers here run their investigation."

"How long is that going to take?" Ritchie asked miserably.

Hansen gave her a kind smile. "Cadet, this isn't some far-flung distant planet, all but unreachable to the authorities, like Oymyakon. We're on a core world now. I promise you, everything is in good hands. All the crime labs they'll be using are close at hand. We won't have to wait long for answers. Just be patient and let the system work."

"I reminded her about Fitz's father," Moreau put in.

Hansen nodded. "That is, of course, always a factor. Nothing is going to happen to Fitz." Then he gave her a strange sort of look. "I thought the two of you were on the outs, anyway. Did I misread the situation?"

"None of that was on my part," Ritchie said, crossing her arms and flinging herself down on her chair. "But even if our roles were reversed, I don't think Fitz would sit idly by while I was carted away in handcuffs."

"No, I don't think he would," Hansen agreed. But then his face was all grim seriousness as he leaned over her, forcing her to meet his eyes before he said, "Ritchie, I know you're going to want to dig into this. I'm telling you not to. That's an order, not a request, understand me?"

"Yes, sir," Ritchie said, somewhat sullenly.

"You can't interfere here like you do back home. The local force won't stand for it. Ritchie, that kind of black mark will absolutely hinder your career. Let the system do the work. Understood?"

"Yes, sir," Ritchie said. Her tone must have been better the second time, because he gave her one last curt nod, then left to head back to his table.

"So, what are we thinking?" Moreau said, sliding into the chair beside Ritchie's. The guardian cadet behind her threw up his hands, then turned to whisper with the two diplomat cadets still lingering there.

"I'm thinking I really hope this was an accident," Ritchie said. Her arms were still crossed and she realized the loud beating sound in her ears was her own angry heartbeat.

"Okay," Moreau said. "Maybe he really did choke, or had some weird allergic reaction. But if not?"

"If not, we do what we always do," Ritchie said.

"And what's that?" Moreau asked, amused.

Ritchie uncrossed her arms and sat forward to fold her hands on the table and put her head close to Moreau's, who was mirroring her posture.

"We work on our list of suspects. Who had motive. Who had means. Who had opportunity. You know," she said.

"Same old, same old," Moreau agreed.

"That should keep us occupied until morning," Ritchie said.

"Okay. So what happens in the morning?" Moreau asked.

"That depends," Ritchie said. "If they let Fitz go, we meet up with him and go over what we've worked out between now and then."

"And if they don't let him go?"

Ritchie sighed, but she had to say it. "If they don't let him go, we find where they're keeping him and we demand they release him."

"Sure," Moreau said, as if Ritchie's plan were the most reasonable thing in the world. "And if they say no? At what point do we reach out to his father? Because, you know, Fitz isn't going to like us doing that. Particularly not you."

"If I have to, I will," Ritchie said. Although she could think of about a million things she'd rather do first.

Starting with busting Fitz out of detainment herself.

But the first plan was still waiting to see whatever the morning held.

8

FITZ HAD SPENT MORE time in various foreign service academy brigs than he probably ought to ever admit. But this was his first time in an actual lockup, being charged with an actual crime.

It was surprisingly nice.

Maybe it was because they weren't sure if they were charging him with anything yet. He wasn't entirely clear what the justification was they were using to hold him. He had been too numb looking down at the body of Kaufmann on the ground at his feet to object when they had cuffed him. And once he was cuffed, he decided he might as well go along with the rest of it.

If he had a single qualm, it was the memory of Ritchie's face, the brief glimpse of it he had gotten before they had dragged him away. All the feelings he was still so numb to, she was feeling for both of them.

He could just imagine the uproar she had unleashed already on his behalf. It only made him feel worse. He didn't deserve half of the loyalty she gave him. He still wasn't in a place where he could return it. He didn't even know when he ever would be.

Fitz sprawled out on the perfectly comfortable bed that sat in the middle of the room, which was nothing at all like a prison cell. It was clean and comfortable. It had a separate, private bathroom with a shower and a door he could close at will. He could feel the breezes blowing over the bed from the open windows behind him. He could smell some sort of night-blooming plant, a sort of honeyish, lavender-y smell that was soft but pleasant.

But he doubted he would be able to sleep, as comfortable as the room was. He got up and headed back to the bathroom to try rinsing his mouth again. He had dry-heaved a lot in the first hour he had spent here. Every time he thought of the look of Kaufmann's dying face and worried it might be poison, he had felt sick, so sick he had tried to make himself throw up. He had only managed to bring up a little bile, but that burned the back of his throat and he couldn't seem to get rid of the taste now.

But surely if he had been poisoned too, he would know it by now. That was something.

He came back out of the bathroom and went to lean out the open window. Presumably something was just beyond his reach, making sure he stayed in this room, but as far as he leaned out, he never encountered it. He didn't know where he was in relation to the dorms, guardian school and diplomat school, or even how far away he was. He could hear voices below as groups of people passed under his window, and somewhere off in the distance, he could hear the thumping bass of a party. For most of the students on Braga, life was carrying on the same as it always did.

Fitz left the window and thought about trying the bed again, but opted instead to open the other door out of his room, the one he had come in through. This opened into a small anteroom between his room and the main corridor. The far door remained closed, and as much as where he was standing looked like an open doorway, he could feel the charge of a force field between him and the anteroom. He put up a hand and slowly moved his palm closer to where he thought the field began.

"I wouldn't do that, if I were you," someone said. Only then did Fitz realize there was a guard in the anteroom, standing between two tall plants that were arranged between the two doors. The guard leaned forward, out of the greenery, and gave Fitz a crooked grin.

"How bad of a shock?" Fitz asked, his hand still raised. "Enough to knock me back on my butt?"

"Enough to knock you out for an hour," the guard said. "Then the medics have to check you out. It's a lot of extra work for me. I'd prefer you didn't."

"And the windows?" Fitz asked, as he put his hands in his pockets.

"You'd have to jump out to test it," the guard told him. "Then you'd get blown back in. You'd be out for more than an hour."

"And you'd have to call two medics," Fitz guessed.

The guard laughed. There was something familiar about that laugh.

"Do I know you?" Fitz asked.

"I wasn't sure you'd remember me," the guard said, stepping out from between the plants to face him. He had dark blonde hair in a tight crewcut and rather unremarkable blue-gray eyes. He was on the short side for a guardian, but wrack his brain as he might, Fitz couldn't place him.

"I'm not sure I do. Sorry," Fitz said.

"No worries. We were only fellow cadets for part of a semester," he said. Then he tapped the nametag on his uniform. "Guardian Cadet Noah Koller, at your service."

"Koller," Fitz said, but the name didn't ring any bells.

"I was a last-year cadet at the Hochberg Foreign Service Academy when you were there," Koller said.

"Okay," Fitz said. It was getting awkward, not remembering this guy. Safest to steer the conversation somewhere else. "So, this chief inspector. What's her name again?"

"Chief Inspector Kasteler," Koller said.

"What's she like?" Fitz asked.

"You have nothing to worry about," Koller said. "Unless you really did kill that guy?"

"Has it been classified a murder?" Fitz asked.

"I guess they're still working that out," Koller said. "Nothing was back from the medical examiner yet, the last I heard. But if you're innocent, you have nothing to worry about. Kasteler is the best there is. Super smart, nothing gets past her. And she's honest, fair. Incorruptible. If someone is trying to frame you for something, they won't get away with it with her on the case."

"That's good to hear," Fitz said. But he couldn't help adding, "I would think on Braga all the crime would be 'stressed out students cut too loose' sorts of things. Is she really that adept at handling frame-ups for murder?"

"She used to work on Jorda," Koller said.

The capital planet, where the seat of government was located. She'd definitely have experience with murder investigations and frame-ups both. Fitz started to relax, if only a little bit.

There was a knock on the door behind Koller, and he turned away from Fitz to open it. He let a tall woman in a crime inspection unit guardian uniform in. She had a tablet in her hands and was studying it even as she stepped into the anteroom to stand before Fitz.

"Hello," Fitz said, when she continued to say nothing at all.

"Hold on," she said distractedly. She reminded him a lot of his buddy Wyss back on Oymyakon, the way her eyes were glued to her tablet. He waited. Then she nodded and cleared something off her screen and opened another document. She scanned it over as if to remind herself of the details, then finally looked up at him. "Shackleton Fitz IV."

"That's me," Fitz said, resisting the urge to find the humor in the situation. Now wasn't the time.

"I have the results back of the medical screening we performed on you during your processing," she said.

"Is that what you were doing?" Fitz said. The officers who had moved him from place to place before finally depositing him in the room with the bed hadn't explained a thing to him.

She blinked at him, then simply said, "yes."

"And the results are… good?"

"You have no trace of any poisons in your system," she said. "And all of your other health indicators are within normal parameters. You're completely healthy."

"*Was* it poison?" he asked.

She blinked again. "Pardon me?"

"Did Nils Kaufmann die because he was poisoned?" he asked.

"I couldn't possibly tell you that," she said as if offended he would even ask.

"Of course. Sorry," Fitz said.

She glared at him, then glared at Koller briefly before disappearing from the room.

"A lot of the med techs are like that," Koller said apologetically. "Particularly on the night shift."

"*Do* they think he was poisoned?" Fitz asked him.

Koller's cheeks colored, and Fitz realized Koller likely wasn't supposed to talk to the prisoner at all, let alone discuss the case with him.

"Forget I asked," Fitz said to let him off the hook.

But Koller rushed to say, "hey, I'd tell you if I knew. No one knows yet. Or at least, no one did when I started my shift here."

"But they're looking into it?" Fitz asked.

"It's one of the first things they check for," Koller said.

"Did you know him? Diplomat Cadet Kaufmann?" Fitz asked.

"Never met him," Koller said. "But by reputation, he's a solid guy. Bright future. No one has a bad word to say against him."

"Yeah, that's what I hear, too," Fitz said with a sigh. He rested a shoulder against the wall on his side of the door. "Not the sort of guy anyone wants dead, right?"

"No way," Koller agreed, a bit too emphatically. Fitz searched his memories again, but if he had ever known this Koller fellow back at the Hochberg Foreign Service Academy, he hadn't made enough of an impression to linger in Fitz's mind.

Which might be a good thing. If he had been a liar or untrustworthy in other ways, Fitz would probably remember him now.

On the other hand, he seemed to describe absolutely everyone in superlative terms. Not everyone could be the greatest ever. Koller probably thought he was being completely honest, but his honest opinions weren't going to be of much use to Fitz if they skewed to the blindly optimistic. He would have to wait until after the shift change and hope the next cadet assigned to guard him was of a more sober, assessing type.

"Hey, Fitz?" Koller said, whispering now for no reason Fitz could tell.

"Yeah, Koller?" Fitz said.

"Is it true that Feena Berweger is your girlfriend?" he asked. But then he didn't even wait for an answer. "That must be just amazing, I am so jealous. She is gorgeous. Absolutely gorgeous. And she just looks like she smells amazing. Does she smell amazing?"

"She has a smell one might describe as amazing," Fitz said. That was as diplomatic a way as he could find to say, "her body secretes mind-altering chemicals that many perceive as their favorite smells and respond to her accordingly."

Then he realized that hadn't been what he should've said at all. He pushed off the wall to stand up and tried to command his brain back to full wakefulness. "She's not my girlfriend, Koller."

"Too late, you gave it away," Koller said, waving an admonishing finger at him. "It's cool. I can keep your secret. I know she's a year ahead of you, so she's here and you're still back at that planet I can never remember the name of. Or pronounce it, even."

"Oymyakon," Fitz offered.

"So you had to break up for a while. It happens," Koller went on as if Fitz hadn't spoken at all. "But come on. Way too many witnesses to your reunion here today, or I guess it was yesterday now. Way too many witnesses, Fitz."

"Have it your way," Fitz said. "If you don't mind, I think I'm going to bed now. Apparently, it's after midnight and all."

"Sure, sure," Koller said, clearly disappointed. Standing guard over a single prisoner while he slept was probably dull as anything, and Fitz knew he was very unlikely to get anything like sleep.

But there was no way he was going to stay up all night chatting about Feena Berweger. No way.

Still, as soon as he darkened the room and stretched out again on the bed to stare up at the ceiling, she was the first thing to pop into his mind.

Just where had she been during the actual dinner? And had Kaufmann taken anything off of her tray before she had disappeared?

Fitz went over it and over it in his mind, but he couldn't recall the details at all. Finally, his exhausted mind just gave it up, and he fell into a restless sleep.

9

THE BUILDING that housed the crime investigation unit looked just like any other building on Braga. Its white marble gleamed brightly in the morning sun, and the surrounding gardens were glistening as the last of the dew evaporated from the leaves and grasses. The flowers were opening up, but their scent was still muted, unable yet to compete with the smell from the cart at the bottom of the building's steps where an older man was selling egg sandwiches and fresh coffee.

The steps up to the door were more numerous, wider, and just generally more imposing than those at the front of the guardian or diplomat schools. But that wide expanse invited sitting, and there were groups of people here and there eating breakfast together.

Ritchie had skipped breakfast herself, anxious to find out at once what was going on. She had dragged a sleepy Moreau out of their dorm room at the first light of dawn, but as early as she had risen, Colonel Hansen had been up even earlier. He had been waiting for them at the door, already dressed in uniform and sipping a mug of his favorite smoky tea. He hadn't said a word, just acted like they had agreed ahead of time to head out to the crime investigation building together first thing in the morning.

It had been a longer walk than Ritchie had expected, and the ankles of her pants were damp from the dew by the time they reached the wider paved road that led to the cluster of government buildings that all faced the same open square. It was the first wide-open space Ritchie had seen on Braga, with no sight of trees or plants anywhere. But the paving stones were immaculate, not marble but some equally beautiful pinkish stone that had glittering sparkles within it.

"Are they expecting us?" Ritchie asked as Colonel Hansen paused at the bottom of the steps as if consulting his implant.

"Inspector Kasteler knows we're coming," he told her.

"Maybe we can grab a quick bite?" Moreau said, looking longingly towards the food cart. The smell of fresh-baked biscuits, eggs, and bacon were strong in the air, and Ritchie's stomach grumbled. But Fitz came first.

Hansen glanced up at the cart. "Why don't you get something for you and Cadet Ritchie and meet us inside? I'll leave our location up on your implant."

"Anything for you?" Moreau asked.

"No, I'm fine," Hansen said, then waved for Ritchie to follow him up those steps to the over-sized doors that stood open to the morning breeze. He navigated the two of them through a maze of corridors and offices to a closed door, where he knocked briskly.

"Come," said Kasteler, and Hansen opened the door to let the two of them in. "I figured I'd see you both today. Maybe not quite so early, though," she said as she stood up from behind her desk and extended a hand to first Hansen and then Ritchie.

"You've been up all night," Hansen guessed.

"I have," Kasteler said. "I just have a few things to finish up here before I can take a quick nap, then get back at it. This is a big case for this station, but nothing we can't handle."

"We won't take up much of your time," Hansen said.

"It's no trouble," Kasteler said. Despite the exhaustion that lined her face, her eyes were bright as she looked at the colonel. "Actually, I'm hoping you can help me with a few details."

There was a knock on the door behind Ritchie, and Hansen turned to open it for Moreau, whose hands were full with two wrapped sandwiches in one hand and two cups of coffee stacked in the other. Ritchie rushed to take her cup before Moreau spilled it while trying to slide into the remaining chair.

"Do you mind if they eat?" Hansen asked. "I know they skipped breakfast, and I doubt they slept any more than you did."

"Feel free," Kasteler said. "Nothing for you? Coffee?" Then something mischievous sparkled in her eyes as she added, "Ravvagge Caravan tea?"

Hansen blinked in surprise. "No, thank you. How did you—"

She smiled as she waved away the question. "I did my research."

"For the case?" Hansen said, still sounding gob smacked.

Moreau nudged Ritchie with her elbow and raised her eyebrows. But whatever this apparent flirtation was about, Ritchie had other things on her mind. She hadn't even unwrapped her sandwich yet, as good as it smelled. "Fitz?" she said, derailing whatever Kasteler had been about to say to Hansen.

"Right," Kasteler said, instantly all business. She picked up her tablet so that they couldn't see her screen from the other side of her desk. She tapped it a few times, then set it down and spun it around to face them. Hansen and Ritchie both leaned over the images and text on the screen, but Moreau in the corner just munched at her sandwich.

"These are the results from the labs we ran on Shackleton Fitz IV last night," she said. The charts meant nothing to Ritchie, but the text under each column was in green. That must mean he was all right.

"You were looking for poison," Hansen guessed. Then he hovered a fingertip over one of the charts. "This reads as in the safe range, but in my experience a reading that high is very suspect."

"In mine as well," Kasteler said. "We checked it again this morning." She took her tablet back to tap it a few times, then showed them another page of charts.

"That looks better," Hansen said, but he didn't sound happy about the result.

"I don't understand," Ritchie said. "What happened to Fitz?"

But neither grownup answered her. Instead, Kasteler tapped the screen of her tablet and brought up another set of charts. These all looked bad, even to Ritchie's eyes. So much red text.

"Nils Kaufmann," Kasteler said.

Hansen clicked his tongue. "It all happened so fast, it's hard to imagine it did so much damage so quickly."

"We don't know exactly what the agent was," Kasteler said. "We have some theories, but it's definitely something rare. We'll need a sample to run more tests before we can be sure."

"You're talking about poison?" Ritchie asked.

"Yes, a poison," Kasteler said.

"You'd need to know who did this to get a sample," Ritchie said.

"I have techs running down the list of all known poisons and comparing the results with what we've sampled from Kaufmann's organs," Kasteler said. "But it's a long list. You are correct, it would be easier to find the poisoner and get the poison than the other way around. But my department is currently working the problem from both ends."

"All the common poisons have already been eliminated, then," Hansen guessed.

"The top million or so," Kasteler said without humor.

"How many does that leave?" Ritchie asked.

"Billions," she said, and rubbed her eyes as if just saying the number exhausted her. "It's a big universe. Even just within the Union of Free Worlds, there are more ways to poison someone than I'd like to imagine."

"But how it worked must narrow that list down. Doesn't it?" Ritchie asked. She felt like she was slowly sinking underwater, farther and farther from the surface with every word out of Kasteler's mouth.

"Well, there is a reason I started with Fitz's levels," she said, and brought those charts back up to her tablet screen.

"Something about how that thing there improved so much overnight?" Ritchie guessed. What she didn't know about poisons would fill a lot of libraries.

"Exactly," Kasteler said.

"Someone gave him the antidote," Hansen said grimly.

"That's the theory at the moment," Kasteler agreed.

"How? When?" Ritchie asked. "We all saw Kaufmann die. Then you arrested Fitz and took him away before anyone else got near him."

"There were a few cadets in close proximity to him. We have a list of them all from the moment Kaufmann started coughing until the minute Fitz was put into his cell here," Kasteler said. "We've reviewed all the security footage from the party and inside the transport and at all points inside this building. So far as we can tell, no one gave Fitz anything, either with or without his consent or knowledge."

"Why does it sound like you're accusing Fitz of something?" Ritchie asked, but they both ignored her question.

"Have they been interrogated yet?" Hansen asked.

"No, because we have a different theory we are working through first," Kasteler said. "As much of a mess as he made of the evidence, we have been able to isolate samples of the food and drink that were on their table last night."

"What was poisoned?" Hansen asked.

"All of it," Kasteler said. "Every bit of food they shared was laced with enough of whatever we're dealing with to kill them both."

"How is that possible?" Ritchie asked.

"We're working on that," Kasteler said. "The cadets who were serving as well as the cook staff are also being questioned."

"If all the food was poisoned, why didn't Fitz collapse first? He was the guest. He ate more," Ritchie said.

"That's why I'm not questioning the cadets who came into contact with Fitz after," Kasteler said. "He clearly had the antidote first."

"How?" Ritchie asked. "The appetizers?"

"Possibly in his drink, but we can't be sure," Kasteler said.

"Because he spilled it," Ritchie said, and sank down into her chair. She didn't like where this was all going.

"Yes, he spilled it," Kasteler said. There was something in her voice that rubbed Ritchie the wrong way.

"You say that like he did it on purpose," Ritchie said.

"If he wanted Kaufmann dead, this would accomplish that. He poisoned everything, knowing he was all the while sipping at the antidote. And once the deed was done, he upended the evidence." Kasteler finished with a shrug.

Ritchie felt like she was about to explode in fury, but Hansen put a hand on her arm, silently commanding her to calm herself.

Then he said to Kasteler, "there is the problem of motive. Cadet Fitz had no prior knowledge of, let alone interaction with, Diplomat Cadet Kaufmann before yesterday afternoon."

"Yes, well," Kasteler said, and shifted her weight in her chair as if the question made her suddenly uncomfortable.

So Ritchie said it for her. "Feena Berweger."

Hansen shot her a puzzled look, but Kasteler was already nodding.

"Yes, Feena Berweger does seem to be the connection between the two of them," she said.

"Frankly, both the Diplomat Cadets Berweger connect every diplomat cadet at that party with every Oymyakon cadet also in attendance. That can't possibly be enough to continue holding Cadet Fitz," Hansen said.

"He's a suspect because he destroyed the evidence," Kasteler said, a warning edge to her voice. She would not have her work questioned, clearly. "For all we know, his intent was to remove evidence of the antidote and poison both."

"It was an accident," Ritchie said.

"It certainly looked that way," Kasteler conceded. "It doesn't mean it was."

"This is crazy," Ritchie said. "Why would Fitz kill anyone over Feena?"

"We know they were in a relationship that ended when she started school here just a few weeks ago," Kasteler said.

"Well," Hansen said, but when he didn't go on, Kasteler just turned her attention back to Ritchie.

"In those few weeks, Feena was seen often in the company of Diplomat Cadet Kaufmann. They are not in the same class, so these meetings were potentially significant."

"They were an item?" Moreau asked, making Ritchie jumped. She had forgotten her buddy was still there behind her, sitting quietly in the corner.

"Fitz and Feena were only spending time together as friends," Ritchie said, although her throat was closing up so tightly she could barely get the words out. "They were never romantically involved."

"Are you sure about that?" Kasteler asked.

"You could ask him," Moreau put in.

"It doesn't matter. Fitz would never kill for her," Ritchie said. She might not be sure about the first thing, but she was definitely sure about the second.

But should she be that sure? She knew what it felt like to spend a few minutes alone with either of the Berweger twins. It left your head spinning. What would it be like, being alone with Feena for all the many minutes, hours, days that Fitz had been over the last semester at the Oymyakon Foreign Service Academy?

And she certainly didn't know a thing about what happened between the two of them over the break. She had been working really hard not to think about that.

"I will allow that you all know Cadet Fitz better than I do," Kasteler said. "I appreciate your words speaking to his character. And for what it's worth, it tracks with my own interactions with him thus far. I would really love to find proof that he's as innocent as you all believe."

"But you're keeping him in custody?" Hansen guessed.

"For the time being," Kasteler said. She didn't quite meet Hansen's eyes. It wasn't the answer she wanted to give him.

Maybe Kasteler's gut really was telling her that Fitz was innocent. Ritchie guessed that was something.

"Have you contacted his father?" Ritchie asked.

"No, but only because he requested that we not do so," Kasteler said. Then she laughed and looked up at Hansen. "Actually, he quoted the legal code to me. You are his chaperone here, in loco parentis, and you've already been informed. Contacting them or not is thus your call. His birth parents only need to be informed by me if he's actually charged with something."

"That sounds like Fitz," Hansen said, also with a little laugh.

But Ritchie just felt sick. "Can I at least see him?"

"Of course," Kasteler said. "But just one of you for now, and in my presence."

Ritchie shot Hansen a pleading look, but he was already lifting his hand to invite her to go.

"Thank you," Ritchie said. Kasteler got up from her chair, and Ritchie realized she had meant they would go right that minute. She started to stand up, only remembering the wrapped sandwich on her lap when she nearly dumped it to the floor. She caught it just in time and handed it to Moreau before following Kasteler out the door.

She had never wanted food less than in that minute. Because not for a minute did she think this was really about Feena. Even if Feena herself was the poisoner, some imagined love triangle was never going to be the real motive.

But the real motive was a complete mystery to her. And until she figured *that* out, anything could be poisoned.

For all she knew, Fitz had been the real target the whole time. And if that were true, she was likely a target as well. The fact that everyone on this core planet had known about the two of them and what they had done on the fringes of known space had creeped her out, even when it seemed like they were being celebrated by everyone.

But what if not everyone thought they were the greatest? What if someone thought they were a threat?

She couldn't even start to figure any of that out until she talked to Fitz. She hurried her steps to keep up with the fast-walking Chief Inspector Kasteler.

10

FITZ WOKE to the sound of voices in the anteroom. Koller, but also someone else. A woman.

Fitz sat up and rubbed the sleep from his eyes. The sun was pouring in through the open windows but hadn't yet reached the head of his bed. When he threw back the blanket, he realized it hadn't burned off the chill to the air yet either. He reached for his tunic first and pulled that on, and then his boots. Then he crossed the room to open the door.

"Breakfast?" he said to Koller, because he could smell eggs and bacon for sure, and he hoped he wasn't imagining there was also coffee. There was indeed a tray of covered dishes and a steaming pot waiting for him, but Koller wasn't holding it.

It was Ritchie.

Fitz instantly felt guilty. He had slept fitfully at first, but then hard. And he has woken surprisingly well-rested, but she clearly had not. And her red-rimmed eyes avoided his, which was puzzling until he realized that, *of course*, this was awkward for her.

He had barely spoken to her in months.

He always forgot that when he saw her. He always only remembered that she was his closest friend. But eventually he would remember how he had poisoned that well.

Now he didn't know what to say. So he said nothing, letting her go first.

"Chief Inspector Kasteler says I can stay with you until you finish breakfast," Ritchie said, as she bent and set the food on the floor outside his door.

"Cool," Fitz said, watching as Koller used a long tool to slide the tray slowly through the force field and into the cell. Fitz sat down on the floor in front of the tray, and Ritchie did the same on the other side of the door.

It *almost* felt like they were eating together, back in the cafeteria on Oymyakon, like they had thousands of times before.

"You look well," Ritchie said, and Fitz felt another spasm of guilt.

"I just woke up," he admitted, taking a sip of the too-hot coffee. He turned his attention to the eggs, but, despite his hunger, took only a very small bite. If his eating was the timetable for their being together, he'd have to eat as slowly as possible.

"I'll be just back here," a woman said, and Fitz finally noticed that Ritchie hadn't come alone. Chief Inspector Kasteler was there, standing beside Guardian Cadet Koller. It was her voice he had heard through the door.

"Thank you," Ritchie said, smiling up over her shoulder before turning back to Fitz. "Do you know you were poisoned?"

Fitz almost choked on his tiny mouthful of scrambled eggs. He swallowed it down, then accidentally followed it with a gulp from the scalding hot coffee. When he finally could speak, he just repeated her word. "Poisoned?"

"They took blood and tissue samples from you?" Ritchie said.

"The tech told me they were fine," Fitz said. "Didn't that mean not poisoned?"

"The poison cleared your system," Ritchie said.

Fitz didn't know what to make of that statement. He had been so paranoid about feeling the effects of a poison, and yet he had been poisoned the whole time and never gotten sick at all? It didn't make any sense.

But what really didn't make any sense was Chief Inspector Kasteler letting the two of them talk about it like this.

Then he looked up at the woman with the salt and pepper hair. She was leaning against the far wall of the anteroom, arms crossed as she pretended to listen to whatever Koller was prattling on about. But her eyes were on Fitz. Always on Fitz.

She wanted to see how he reacted to what Ritchie had to say. That's why she had let Ritchie come at all.

Did Ritchie realize? He couldn't tell.

"Kaufmann and I were both poisoned?" he asked.

"Yes."

"Just us two?"

"I guess so."

"Why?" Fitz asked.

"I have thoughts," Ritchie mumbled darkly. Fitz fought the urge to bark out a laugh. He could tell what was going on now, just from the look on her face. Even though she was staring down at the sides of her boots as she sat cross-legged on the floor, he could tell.

Ritchie's theories were being ignored.

"What's the official theory?" he asked.

"Feena Berweger," Ritchie said, still not looking at him.

"They think Feena poisoned us both?" Fitz sputtered. "Why?"

"No, they think—" Ritchie started to say.

But Kasteler interjected a quiet, "careful."

Ritchie pivoted on the floor to look up at Kasteler. "You have to tell him if he's a suspect. Don't you?"

"I'm a suspect? But you just said I was poisoned," Fitz said, setting his fork down. He was suddenly not remotely hungry.

"Are you finished?" Kasteler asked, nodding at his tray.

"I don't know. Is *this* poisoned?" he asked, looking down at the eggs, bacon and toast, each in their own little square bowl.

"You are quite safe here, Cadet Fitz. Even if you are a target, no one can get to you here," Kasteler assured him.

But Fitz felt far from reassured. "First of all, if I have enemies willing to poison me, they are powerful people who can get to me wherever I am. So thank you very much, but I don't feel safe here.

Sorry. I mean, if the Berwegers are involved, do you even know what that means?"

"Feena Berweger isn't a suspect," Kasteler said.

"Then why did you mention her?" Fitz asked.

"They think she's the motive," Ritchie said miserably.

"Oh," Fitz said. "Yeah, that makes sense."

"What?" Ritchie gasped, eyes wide with shock.

"From their point of view, it makes sense," Fitz said, gesturing past her towards Kasteler. "Come on, Ritchie. You know I'd never kill for Feena Berweger."

"I don't know what I know," Ritchie said, her eyes back on her boots. She started picking at a loose thread in the stitching around a buckle.

"You know that," Fitz said with complete certainty.

"You said 'first of all'," Kasteler reminded him. She sounded amused. "Was there a second of all?"

"What?" Fitz said, then remembered where he had gotten sidetracked. "Oh, right. First you tell me I'm a suspect, then you tell me I'm a target. *I* thought I was here as a witness."

"No, you didn't," Kasteler said, still amused.

But Fitz ignored her, staying on his point. "So, which is it?"

"Forget them," Ritchie said, finally looking up at him. Her eyes were still wide, but intense now. She wanted desperately to be working this case. "Tell me what happened."

"I went over the whole story last night five times with five different inspectors," Fitz sighed.

"Tell *me*," Ritchie said.

"Well, you were there," Fitz said. "We arrived for the dinner—"

"No," Kasteler interrupted, much to Fitz's irritation. "You need to back up. Start with your tour yesterday afternoon at the diplomat school."

"Why?" Fitz asked.

"Start with the moment Feena Berweger interrupted the tour," Kasteler pressed.

Fitz looked up at Ritchie. Her fingers were still toying with that loose thread, but she was more or less looking at Fitz now.

He really didn't want to talk about Feena in front of Ritchie. He had avoided that for months now. He tried to catch her eyes, tried to implore her to remember that this had all been a mission Colonel Hansen had given him, but she didn't acknowledge him at all.

But he could tell she was listening.

"I understand the rumor mill has it that Feena Berweger and I are a hot item or whatever," he said, stabbing at his eggs with his spork, breaking the perfect curdles into a slurry. "But we're just friends. Our families are close. We both spent the break on Jorda, and we spent a lot of time together. That was it."

"A lot of people saw her say hello to you," Kasteler said. Fitz gritted his teeth at the persistent amused tone to her voice, but decided not to engage with it.

"Feena is demonstratively affectionate. That doesn't change anything I just said," Fitz said. "And I'm not even contradicting what everyone thinks is true. I know they all believe it. I never cared enough to argue about it. So when everyone saw Feena run to say hello to me, and drag me away from the tour to walk alone with me, I knew what everyone was thinking. I just didn't care to correct anyone."

Ritchie's head was still down, and her brown curls covered her face, but he could see the tips of her ears reddening.

"We arrived at the lawn party together, and Nils Kaufmann saw us together. He didn't approach me or speak to me, so I don't know what he was thinking in that moment. But he was watching us."

"He liked Feena," Ritchie said. "That's what I've heard."

"Maybe," Fitz said with a shrug. "Feena didn't feel the same. None of that has anything to do with me."

"What happened at the dinner?" Ritchie asked.

"We were assigned to sit together. It wasn't awkward past the first minute. Kaufmann was a cool guy, and we were having an interesting conversation when all of a sudden he just started coughing," Fitz said.

Now it was Ritchie interrupting him. "Back up. This was poison. Focus on the food."

"I had a few appetizers before I sat down with Kaufmann," Fitz said. "I guess those were safe?"

"Or they contained—" Ritchie started to say, but Kasteler cut her off.

"Continue," she ordered Fitz.

"Do I have to remember what I ate?" he asked, setting aside the watery sludge that had been his eggs.

"Just tell us what details you remember," she said.

"I told all this last night," Fitz said again, but closed his eyes and tried to summon up images. "I had a few squares of the cheese first. I don't remember the server who gave me those. Just some diplomat cadet. Then I had a toast thing." He opened his eyes and looked at Ritchie. "Feena gave me that one."

"Oh," Ritchie said, looking completely miserable. "That could be… never mind." She glanced back towards Kasteler, and Fitz could tell she was policing her own words now.

"Feena wasn't the server at our table, though. It was just Kaufmann and I at our table, and I honestly didn't really look up at anyone who brought us food. I just know it wasn't Feena, and it wasn't Finn."

"You followed the protocol?" Ritchie asked.

It took him a minute to grasp what she was asking. "Yes," he said. "Someone would bring a tray of food, and I would pick the items. Then Kaufmann would take the first bite. Then I would eat as much as I wanted, and he would finish it off. Except the soup. After he tasted it, he didn't have more. Honestly, I don't remember everything we ate. Wings and fish and soup, for sure. Beyond that? I don't recall."

"What did you drink?" Ritchie asked.

"Whatever was in those cups. Some dry, fruity thing," Fitz said.

"You didn't know what it was?" Ritchie asked.

"Did you?" he countered.

"No," she said. "So if it tasted off, I wouldn't know. I didn't have a baseline."

"Me neither," Fitz said. But then he shook his head. "That can't be the thing, Ritchie. If Kaufmann and I were both poisoned, it wouldn't have been the drink. We didn't share that. In fact, I never even saw him take a sip from his cup at all."

"That's not good, Fitz," Ritchie said, sounding more miserable than ever.

"How is that not good? Surely by now you've tested all the food.

You must know what was poisoned," Fitz said. He looked from Ritchie to Kasteler.

"You knocked over both the glasses," Ritchie said.

"What difference does that make?" Fitz asked.

Ritchie said nothing.

"The agent we're looking for likely would've persisted longer in a container such as those glasses than it did spread out over the table-cloth in a quickly drying puddle," Kasteler told him.

"What agent are we talking about?" Fitz asked.

"Go ahead, cadet," Kasteler said. "Tell him."

Ritchie looked up at Fitz. "They think the food was poisoned. All of it. And that the antidote was in your glass. Because you didn't share those."

Fitz felt a sudden chill running up his spine. He had assumed they were just holding him as a witness. That they wanted to be sure he didn't talk to others and contaminate his story.

He had thought he'd be getting out of here soon.

"So I'm a suspect," he said slowly. But even when he said the words out loud, they wouldn't sink into his brain.

"You picked the food you both ate. It might've been marked some-how," Ritchie said. "You had the antidote in the glass, which you then knocked over when the poison started taking effect. To some, it looks like you destroyed the evidence."

Which, of course, was what they had charged him with. Why had he thought that was just a pretext to move him?

"What is happening?" he said numbly.

"Time's up, Cadet Ritchie," Kasteler said, pushing away from the wall.

"I'm going to fix this, Fitz," Ritchie said earnestly. "I'm going to figure out what's really going on."

"I believe that's my job," Kasteler said as she extended a hand to help Ritchie to her feet.

But Ritchie stayed where she was, sitting across from Fitz.

"You believe me, right? That I would never hurt anyone on account of Feena?" he asked.

"I know you didn't," Ritchie said. "I'm going to prove it. I won't leave this planet until you're declared innocent."

"All right, that's enough of that," Kasteler said, and grabbed Ritchie's wrist herself to force her back to her feet.

"I won't stop," Ritchie cried back over her shoulder as she was propelled out of the room.

"I know," Fitz yelled after her, but she was gone.

"Man, you are the luckiest guy in the universe, aren't you?" Koller said, shaking his head in bemusement.

"She's just a friend," Fitz grumbled, turning his attention back to the unappetizing remains of his breakfast.

"Everyone's just a friend to you," Koller shot back. "Hey, I have friends too. Most people do. What we don't have is friends like that one. I believe every word she said. She's really not leaving here without you, is she?"

Fitz didn't answer. One by one, he put the covers back on the dishes and pushed the tray back out to Koller. Someone was either trying to kill him or was trying to frame him. Neither option was great for him.

Either one of them could mean the end of his career. And if that was over, his friendship with Ritchie would have to follow.

Because even if she was willing to remain outside his cell until he was set free, there was no way he was going to let her jeopardize her future for him. No way.

11

BY THE TIME RITCHIE, Moreau and Colonel Hansen got back to the dormitory, the other cadets were already dispersed between the two schools. The breakfast room was still a wreck of crumb-laden plates and stacks of empty coffee cups, and there was no sound of voices anywhere inside the building or in the gardens outside. Birds were calling, and a few insects were beginning to whir and chitter, but it was otherwise sleepily quiet.

That, plus the warmth of the breeze as it blew through the common rooms, reminded Ritchie just how little she had slept the night before.

"You were both scheduled for classes at the guardian school today," Colonel Hansen said to them as they stood in the main hall, hovering between the corridor that led to the back patio and the stairs that led up to the rooms. "I can reschedule you for the day after tomorrow, but I can only do that once. You'll have to go to classes at the diplomat school tomorrow for sure. There isn't any more time for me to knock things back to."

"I understand," Ritchie said. "I just need a day."

"Me too," Moreau said, although she didn't sound tired at all.

"Take some time to rest, then," Hansen said. "Message with your friends who live on Braga if you like. You're going to lose your free day later if you take it today."

"Okay," Ritchie said numbly. She wasn't sure calling Guy was what she wanted to do right now. In fact, it felt like the opposite of what she wanted.

"What you absolutely must not do is interfere in Chief Inspector Kasteler's investigation," Hansen said firmly. "If you mess up here, I can't protect you, Ritchie. You either, Moreau. If you get caught interfering, it could end your careers. And I would really hate to see that."

"We won't," Moreau said, putting an arm around Ritchie and leading her towards the stairs. "We're just going to take it easy today. We have another meet and greet scheduled for this evening, meeting the faculty at the guardian school. We'll be there for that. But in the meantime, we're going to rest up."

"That sounds like a wise plan," Hansen said, but the way he said it, it sounded more like a command.

Moreau just nodded, then led Ritchie up the stairs. They went into their shared room and sat down on their unmade beds. Moreau put her chin in her hands and waited for Ritchie to speak.

"I have to do something," Ritchie said. "And a nap isn't it."

"Are you going to send a message to Guy? Tell him what's going on?" Moreau asked.

"If I did that, he'd be here in a heartbeat," Ritchie said, then sighed. "I don't think Guy being here would be helpful."

"I don't know. He sounded like a handy guy to have around in an investigation back on the boat," Moreau said.

Ritchie remembered that adventure. Moreau had been with the group diving to the underwater city at the time, but Ritchie and Guy had remained on the boat. Ritchie didn't like being underwater, and Guy only liked oceans because that's where sailing ships were. So they had been alone when pirates had come aboard looking to steal the valuables yachts like Guy's tended to have on board.

"He was handy in a fight," Ritchie conceded. "But this isn't a fight. And he gets weird when I talk about Fitz."

"Can you blame him?" Moreau asked.

"What's that supposed to mean?" Ritchie asked.

"Nothing. I get it," Moreau said. "This is all about Fitz, and if Guy were here, he'd immediately see the obvious."

"What's that?" Ritchie asked.

"That the best way to protect you is to get you away from Fitz and his problems," Moreau said.

"I'm not doing that," Ritchie said.

"I know," Moreau said emphatically. "So, what are you and I going to do?"

"I want to look around that school some more," Ritchie admitted. "Not part of a tour, not in a class. I just want to nose around."

"Me too," Moreau said with a sly grin. "Let's go."

They crossed the maze of gardens back to the lawn and patio that extended out of the diplomat school library. There was no indication that this was a crime scene. There were no inspectors working the site, no areas cordoned off, nothing.

There wasn't even any sign remaining of the party. All the tables, floating chandeliers, heaters and other decorations were gone. It was just an expanse of somewhat weathered marble and a lawn of what looked like untouched grass.

"I hope they got all the evidence before they took it all down," Ritchie said.

"I'm sure they did," Moreau assured her. "These people are professionals, remember?"

"So they keep telling me," Ritchie said. The offices had looked efficient when they had passed through them. The inspectors collecting evidence and witness testimony the night before had struck her as completely competent. She couldn't fault anything she had seen happening.

And yet, if they were still considering Fitz to be a suspect, they were still doing something wrong.

"You didn't really think we were going to find a physical clue that the inspectors missed," Moreau said, not a question.

"No, I didn't," Ritchie said. "I want to talk to the cadets about Nils Kaufmann. Someone must know who might want him dead."

They climbed the steps to the patio, then passed through the trees into the library itself. It was midmorning and classes were in session, but there was still a spattering of cadets studying in the library, including one familiar face.

Ritchie nudged Moreau, then pointed across the room to Nika Heim. Heim had graduated from the Oymyakon Foreign Service Academy just the year before, but Ritchie had gotten to know her a bit during their time during extreme environment tactical training. Or what had been meant to be EETT before the murder of Heim's buddy had derailed everything.

Heim had struck Ritchie as honest, forthright, and observant, if a bit on the shy side.

Ritchie and Moreau approached the table where Heim had her head bent over a tablet, waiting for her to notice them first. It took her a minute, but when she saw who was standing over her, she gave them both a tired sort of smile.

"Aren't you supposed to be auditing a class now?" she asked.

"Did you hear about last night?" Ritchie asked.

"Oh, right. Fitz," Heim said, nodding, then motioned for them to join her at her table. She moved a few older model tablets, some positively antique, out of the way first. Then she said, "I was there, actually. I was one of the servers. But nowhere near that end of the patio. Do you know what happened?"

"Not exactly," Ritchie said. "How well do you Nils Kaufmann?"

"Not well," Heim said. "A lot of people here are taking his death really hard. I didn't know him well, but it feels like everyone in the upper three classes did, or felt like they did. He will be missed, that's for sure."

"Someone must have felt differently," Moreau said, and Ritchie flinched. That was too direct an observation in her view. But Heim just shrugged.

"Maybe?" Then another thought struck her, and she leaned forward over the table, motioning for them to put their faces close to hers. "Is it the Berwegers? Because I can't begin to tell you how much I hate the fact that they're both here. It makes me so nervous. Beyond that. I don't really have the words."

"I know," Ritchie said. "It's not great for anybody. Doesn't anyone here realize what they are yet?"

"No. I think we need you and Fitz here to straighten things out," Heim said.

"Tall order," Moreau said.

Heim blushed. Then something across the room caught her attention, and she started waving her arm, imploring someone to join them. "Dauss knew Kaufmann pretty well. She's really the one you should be talking to. Cadet captain!" she said when Dauss drew close enough to hear.

"Cadet Heim," Dauss said, giving her a little nod. "And Cadet Ritchie and Cadet Moreau. I wasn't expecting either of you until tomorrow."

"We'll be back for classes tomorrow," Ritchie promised her. "We have a free day today."

Dauss frowned, as that clearly didn't match the schedule she had been given. Ritchie could see her eyes start to dart as she consulted her implant.

"We moved some things around," Ritchie quickly explained. "We wanted to talk to everyone about what happened last night."

"Oh, I see," Dauss said, but she didn't sound pleased.

"We're not interfering with the investigation," Moreau said.

"We're really not," Ritchie said. "I'm just trying to understand what's going on."

"Of course," Dauss said, and sat down in the free chair with a gentle smile. "Your friend is implicated. I understand."

"I'm afraid he might actually be a target," Ritchie said.

"Why ever for?" Dauss asked.

"You know what he and Ritchie have been up to," Moreau said. "It's the kind of thing that makes enemies."

"Two days ago I would say that sounded crazy, but since we've arrived here, it's like everyone knows everything we've ever done," Ritchie said.

"You have many admirers," Dauss said.

"And maybe a few people who would rather see us gone. Or at least Fitz," Ritchie said.

Dauss frowned. She folded her hands together on the tabletop, a calm gesture, but one Ritchie suspected she had learned to use in place of a more fidgety one.

"Who would want Kaufmann dead?" Ritchie asked her.

Dauss looked startled at the question. "No one," she said. "Honestly. The thought boggles my mind. He is far and away the brightest mind to come through here in decades. But he's not remotely stuck up about it. Did you never speak with him?"

Ritchie shook her head.

"That is a shame," Dauss said. "Anyone who spoke to Kaufmann came away believing they were the one doing amazing things, not Kaufmann. He remembered details about people and always knew just what to say. Not the usual mindless flattery which, I admit, is what most cadets take away from the classes here. He was really good at talking to people."

"He must've rubbed someone the wrong way," Moreau said.

"No, I don't think so," Dauss said.

"Someone wanted him dead," Ritchie said, but before Dauss could respond, Moreau was interjecting.

"What do you think of the Berwegers?"

"The Berwegers," Dauss said slowly, as if the question had caught her off guard and she needed a minute to come up with a response. "The Berwegers are… hard to trust. But frankly, your friend Fitz has put himself in the same category. He clearly is their ally."

"I know it looks that way," Ritchie said. "I promise quite the opposite is true."

"Well, I'm sure I don't know," Dauss said, far too diplomatically.

"What do you think happened?" Moreau asked.

"I think Nils was an innocent victim," Dauss said. "I think your friend Fitz and his friends the Berwegers are caught up in things far bigger than this school, and they brought a bit of that world in here with them."

"Fitz didn't hurt anyone, I promise you," Ritchie said.

"Maybe not," Dauss said, again clearly saying what she thought Ritchie wanted to hear, not what she was actually thinking herself.

It was maddening.

"What do you know about poisons?" Moreau asked casually.

"Almost nothing, I'm sure," Dauss said mildly.

"Come on," Moreau said. "Seriously?"

"Poison is a weapon. Perhaps you should speak to a guardian. Weapons are their purview."

"But poison is a diplomat's weapon," Ritchie said.

Dauss looked offended, almost to the point of anger. "That's not what is taught here."

"Historically," Ritchie clarified. "Does no one study it?"

"If anyone did, I'm sure it would be your friends the Berwegers," Dauss said as she got to her feet.

"We just want a little help here," Moreau said.

"Cadets, you are in a library," Dauss said. At first Ritchie thought she was going to admonish them about the noise they were making, but that wasn't what Dauss meant. "If you want to learn more about the historical use of poison by diplomats as a weapon, this would be the place for that research. But I'm afraid I simply do not have a time to help you."

Then she turned on her heel and marched away.

"I'm afraid I don't either," Heim said with a sympathetic grimace. "I can help you get started using the systems, but I really need to focus on my own research right now. I'm really behind declaring a topic for my paper."

"It's fine. We've got it," Moreau assured her.

"We do?" Ritchie asked as the two of them got up and crossed the room from Heim's table to the central desk.

"Sure," Moreau said with a shrug. "It's a library. It's built to impart knowledge. How hard could it be?"

Ritchie shared her grin. That certainly sounded like solid reasoning to her.

But as the hours ticked by with no answers emerging from the growing stacks of tablets around them, she started to doubt that premise.

And the value of her own plan.

And pretty much everything about the universe and all it contained.

12

FITZ SAT ALONE on the edge of his bed, eating a bowl of beef stew with fluffy, herby dumplings. The broth was rich, there were at least three kinds of mushroom mixed in with the beef that was probably raised somewhere on this planet and not transported across interstellar distances to get to his bowl. But it was the dumplings that really did it for him. They were some magical combination of potato and flour and definitely real butter.

Yes, it was undoubtedly the dumplings he hated the most. Because he wanted to be moody and depressed now that he was about to start his second night in lockup. Delicious food wasn't letting him do that. It was annoying.

He heard voices in the anteroom just as he was scraping the last of the broth out of the bottom of the bowl. He put it back on the tray with the plastic cutlery, then brought it to the door he had left standing open.

As anxious as he had been to have someone other than Cadet Koller to talk with, the young woman who had taken over for him had refused to answer any of his questions. She hadn't even told him her name. And Chief Inspector Kasteler had never come back. Neither had anyone else. He had spent a whole day's worth of hours pacing the nice room and wishing he knew what was going on outside of it.

"Shift change?" Fitz said conversationally as he set his tray on the floor within reach of the implement that could reach through the force field. The young woman just glared at him. But then she went out the door into the corridor beyond.

But the cadet who was taking her place was a familiar face. Although the platinum color of his hair was probably his more memorable feature.

"Blaser!" Fitz said. "Good to see you, man."

"I had to twist some arms to get this assignment, but I really wanted to talk to you," Blaser said.

"What's up?" Fitz asked. Blaser had worked with Fitz and Ritchie before, first helping them find his missing buddy Leodegrance Kung so they could clear him of suspicion in the murder of Cadet Captain Jeger, and just the year before helping them find out who had killed Cadet Captain Milla Wyder.

Cadet captains at Oymyakon Foreign Service Academy had a frighteningly high death rate, Fitz realized. He was doubly grateful he hadn't been picked for that role now that he was a last-year. Although Blaser had come through it all right.

"I don't have any inside knowledge of what went down at that dinner party," Blaser told him. "I wasn't even there. But I've heard enough to be concerned. Is this a Berweger issue? Should we be doing something?"

"Who's we?" Fitz asked.

"All of us who know what they really are," Blaser said.

"So I'm not the only one who feels like they are apex predators swimming a bit too freely in the prey pool," Fitz said.

"I don't actually know how any of the diplomat cadets feel, but there's quite a few of us at the guardian school who are worried," Blaser said. "It's a little tricky trying to keep tabs on them."

"We should network with a few of the diplomat cadets, then," Fitz said. "I saw a few friendly faces during the tour, people who would surely help. Your buddy Kung, just to start."

"Every time I message him, he just tells me how colossally busy he is," Blaser grumbled.

"Do you think he's ducking you?" Fitz asked.

Blaser pondered it. "No, I don't think so."

"Me neither," Fitz said.

"We were close at the academy, and it wasn't all that long ago," Blaser said.

"The diplomat cadets seem pretty academically focused. Maybe even too much so."

"Maybe," Blaser agreed. "But how do the Berwegers factor into that?"

"Everyone so focused on their own coursework is probably giving them too much leeway," Fitz said. "I'm just speculating. How much trouble could they possibly have gotten into already? It's only been a few weeks."

"A few weeks, and one murder," Blaser said.

"So you know about the poison," Fitz guessed.

"I've heard a few different stories, but poison is a common thread in all of them."

"Well, and you can imagine how much I hate to admit this, but as best as I can recall, neither of the Berwegers were anywhere near our table when Kaufmann collapsed. They weren't there at any point during the dinner. Feena brought me over to the table and gave me one of the toast things from her tray, but that was it. She disappeared when Kaufmann turned up."

"That doesn't make them innocent," Blaser said. "Maybe the opposite, really. You and I both know they like to get others to do the actual dirty work for them."

"That's true," Fitz said.

"With a few exceptions, everyone serving that dinner was a first-year diplomat cadet. They all had classes with either one or both of the twins. Finn and Feena had access to all of them."

"All of them? You have lists? Proof?" Fitz asked.

Blaser shook his head. "No, just a hunch."

"We need diplomat cadet help to figure out the schedules and the likeliest suspects," Fitz said.

"I can try reaching Kung again. If I mention your name, he might realize how serious this is," Blaser said.

"Sure, you could try that," Fitz said. But a thought was bugging him. "I just assumed Ritchie was there already."

"Oh, she is," Blaser said. "I assumed you already knew that."

"I've been stuck in this room all day," Fitz said, raising his hands to invite Blaser to take in his confined, if opulent, surroundings.

"Right. Well, she and Moreau skipped out of their scheduled auditing classes and went to the diplomat school library instead. I don't know what they're up to. I can find out, but not until I get off shift," Blaser said.

"In the morning," Fitz guessed, and Blaser nodded. "Don't worry about it. I'm sure Ritchie will be back here by then, demanding my release again."

"Why *are* they holding you?" Blaser asked.

"Just being thorough," Fitz said, more cheerfully than he felt.

Blaser scowled at him. "If they were being thorough, they'd have the Berwegers in here and not you."

"You can't exactly blame them. The Berwegers keep skating out of suspicion for anything. Officially, they've never done a thing wrong. Why arrest them?" Fitz shrugged.

"Well, I, for one, would feel a lot better if you and Ritchie were working this case," Blaser said.

"We are," Fitz said.

"I meant together. In the same place. Right now."

"I'm sure I'll be out soon," Fitz said. "I'm just waiting for the wheels of bureaucracy to finish turning."

"Maybe," Blaser said. "Or maybe we can make something happen faster."

"Guardian Cadet Blaser, are you offering to bust me out of a crime investigation unit detention cell?" Fitz asked, amused. Blaser had always been a follow-the-rules guy. But Fitz could see on Blaser's face now that he absolutely was not joking.

"Like I said, I'm not the only guardian cadet who's worried about this," Blaser said. "If the authorities aren't looking into the twins, at least you and Ritchie should."

"Thanks for that vote of confidence," Fitz said. "No, seriously. I mean, we've never actually managed to pin anything on them."

"Not for lack of trying," Blaser said.

Fitz just shrugged. "People tell me Chief Inspector Kasteler is honest and fair. I'll stay in her hands, at least until she proves herself otherwise."

"The offer stands," Blaser said.

"Yeah, thanks," Fitz said. "I expect I'll be out by morning, but if I'm not, definitely get with Kung and with Ritchie and Moreau. They'll know what to do. They probably have that list of diplomat cadets that might have been influenced by the Berwegers already."

"I hope so," Blaser said.

"Me too," Fitz said.

He went back into his room and sat on the bed, but he wasn't remotely tired. He was restless. He wanted to be out there with Ritchie and Moreau, figuring out just what had happened that night. Now that Blaser had mentioned it, it did feel wrong that no one was looking into the Berwegers. Sure, they'd have no official reason to, but protocol aside, it ought to be done.

And he ought to be a part of doing it. It was his job. Quite aside from his role on Colonel Hansen's task force, it was feeling more and more like this was what he was working to become a guardian to do. They had to be stopped, and he was better equipped than most to do it.

Fitz laid back on the pillow and threw an arm across his eyes.

If they didn't let him out in the morning, he had only one card left to play. Contacting his father. Once that happened, he would be out of detention before the call was even over.

But there would be consequences.

He really hoped he didn't have to play that card.

13

RITCHIE COULDN'T SLEEP. As much as she and Moreau had toiled all the hours of the day researching poisons and learning tons—if nothing useful—her brain really wanted to keep going over all the details. She wanted to talk to someone, to keep discussing things until some new lead emerged.

But Moreau was snoring softly on the bed next to hers, and Ritchie didn't want to wake her.

As quietly as she could, she threw back her covers and pulled on her clothes, carrying her boots until she was at the bottom of the stairs and well away from any sleeping cadets. Once she had them on, she crept out the back door and down the patio steps, past the expanse of lawn until she could wander in the hedges.

Well, she'd been wanting to do that since they arrived. She wasn't going to enjoy it now the way she might have if she'd done it on the first day, but it might calm her mind enough to let her sleep.

There was no moon in the sky above, but the stars were bright, and the hedges themselves were filled with little lights that glowed from within the depths of the leaves. Most of that light was directed down to illuminate the cobblestone paths. The air was still warm, warmer than it had been the night before, and the scents of night-blooming flowers were softer than the daytime blooms.

Occasionally, Ritchie would walk through a cloud of fine mist that coated the leaves and blades of grass around her. It had a sweet herby smell, and even tasted minty on her lips. She supposed this was some sort of irrigation system, although she couldn't tell just where it was coming from. She hoped it was safe for humans, whatever she was tasting.

She took a side passage off the main path and found herself in an enclosed alcove surrounded by hedges. A single stone bench sat between two large potted plants with stiff, upward-thrusting leaves that put her in mind of over-sized leeks. But it was a dead-end, and she didn't really want to sit down. She wanted to keep walking.

She turned to go back the way she'd come, but jumped as she realized she was no longer alone.

"Finn Berweger," she said, certain she recognized the silhouette's posture. The height was pretty distinctive.

And indeed he stepped forward into better light and she saw it was him. He was wearing a dark-colored hoodie over his diplomat cadet uniform, but he pushed back the hood as he moved closer to her so she could see his face.

"Murdina Ritchie," he said, his voice all warmth, a low rumble that echoed in her chest.

"I was just..." she said, pointing back the way she'd come, then trying to step around him.

"Ritchie, don't go," he said. "I know you're probably suspicious of me because of what happened. I had nothing to do with it, but I'm sure you'd want proof of that."

"How could you possibly prove that?" Ritchie asked, turning to face him despite her intention to leave.

"All right, you got me," he said, raising his hands as if in surrender. "If it helps, I know Fitz wasn't involved either."

"Well, can you prove *that*?" Ritchie asked.

"I'm working on it," he said.

"Sure you are," Ritchie scoffed.

He just shrugged. "Again, I understand your scepticism. But I really do feel for Fitz in this. He comes from a powerful family, just like Feena and I come from a powerful family. People are always going to try to bring us down."

"You're honestly saying this to me?" Ritchie asked. "Like I don't know you've actually done a lot of what you've been accused of?"

Finn laughed self-deprecatingly. "Yeah, ironic, right? I guess I always know in my heart that you're going to turn around someday."

"You think I'm going to take your side?" Ritchie asked. "Are you forgetting I was right there when you tried to destroy the evidence of the murder your parents were a part of? And then there's what you did to me…"

But she really didn't want to talk about that. She pushed him out of her way and started following the path back the way she'd come.

But he caught up, falling into step beside her. "I'm sorry about that. Truly," he said. Ritchie just scoffed. "No, honestly. I crossed a line, I know that. I don't always remember to use my powers only for good."

"Are you kidding me right now?" Ritchie demanded, stopping in the middle of the path to face him.

"No, I'm being completely honest," he said, raising his hands again. "Look, your friend and my sister are tangled up with each other in a way that I don't exactly understand. It baffles me. I don't know how you feel about it, but maybe you're confused about it too. But my point is, they seem to care about each other. And Feena is my sister. I want what's best for her."

"And in this case, that's what exactly?" Ritchie asked.

"I guess it's Fitz not being accused of a crime he didn't commit," he said. "She's very upset about it."

"Is she," Ritchie said, not quite a question. She doubted it very much.

But Finn's eyes were wide and sincere. "Yes. She is."

Ritchie took a deep breath, but all she smelled on the air was the scent of jasmine and the remains of that minty spray. Nothing that she usually smelled when Finn was putting the whammy on her. Maybe he really was being honest.

But she'd be a fool to believe that.

"You were researching poisons all day," Finn said.

"I was," Ritchie admitted.

"Did you learn anything?"

"No," she said.

"Wouldn't it be easier to find out who did this first? The number of people who came in contact with that food is a far more manageable number than all the poisons in the known universe," he said. His eyes were sparkling at her, but she didn't think he was teasing her, exactly.

"I will be auditing classes at the diplomat school tomorrow," Ritchie said. "I'm hoping to get a list of suspects started then. It's a little tricky doing this at a school where I know so few of the cadets."

"You managed it before, when you were still new at the academy," Finn reminded her.

"I had Fitz's help," Ritchie said.

"Well, now you have mine, if you'll take it," he said.

"You know I can't trust you," she said. "Anything you told me, I'd have to verify myself, and assume you were spoon-feeding me, so I would draw the conclusion you want me to draw."

"Well, the offer stands," he said, and swept an arm, inviting her to keep walking with him.

Ritchie hesitated, but then started walking with him deeper into the maze of hedges. If he was going to take no for an answer so easily, perhaps this wasn't the dumbest thing she'd done lately.

"So you're auditing diplomat classes tomorrow, you said," Finn said conversationally. "Does that mean you're looking to attend next year? You know, we only get about a third of the cadets who come out of the academies. Most go to the guardian school instead."

"I'll probably be one of the 'most'," she said. "I don't think I'm cut out to be a diplomat."

"Oh, nonsense," he said. "It's in your blood."

"I don't think it works that way," Ritchie said. "I'm guessing your family doesn't work that way either, or your parents wouldn't have felt they had to doctor you and your sister so much."

"Ouch," Finn said with a little flinch, but then he smiled. "You're not pulling any punches today, are you?"

"You're the one who insists on walking with me," she said with a shrug. But her heart was pounding. How hard could she push him before he pushed back? And what would that look like?

She really shouldn't be alone with him.

"Still, your father was highly talented, no doubt. But you've proven yourself just as skilled, haven't you?"

"I don't think so," she said.

"Come, now. You were given an assignment as an acting diplomat while still at the academy. And not even as a last-year cadet. Do you know how rare that is?"

"It was impressed on me," she said. "It was a special assignment. I got it because of personal connections to the subjects involved, not from skill."

"I think it was both," Finn said, smiling at her with his eyes again.

She wished he'd stop doing that.

"I think my future is in the guardian school," she said. "I hope it doesn't hurt your feelings, but you being in the diplomat school is a part of that decision-making calculus."

"Why would that hurt my feelings?" he said blandly. "I know you'll always choose Fitz first. I have no delusions about that."

"It sounds like you have delusions about *something*," Ritchie said. "Do you mind explaining that remark?"

"Well, like I said, I don't get what's happening between my sister and Fitz," he said. There was something in his voice, a core of sincerity that she actually believed wasn't feigned. She stopped walking again to look at him, which was a mistake.

Pheromones weren't his only super power. His eyes did something, too.

But that was the second time he had mentioned not understanding what was between his sister and Fitz.

"Are you trying to ask me if I know what's really going on between them?" Ritchie asked.

Even by starlight, she could see the flush of color that touched his cheeks.

"Do you?" he asked.

"How openly do you want to talk about this?" she asked. "Because if I have to pretend that you and your sister aren't up to something on behalf of your parents and probably a bunch of other people I don't know, I can't really do that anymore."

"Neither should we pretend that Colonel Hansen hasn't told you lots of stories to convince you that my sister and I need to be watched carefully," he countered.

Ritchie narrowed her eyes at him. "Again, I remind you that I caught you burning evidence."

"Evidence of a long-past childhood indiscretion," he said, "by cadets who went on to have superlative careers."

"It was a dead kid," she said.

"Haven't you ever done something for the sake of your family that you did even though you thought it was wrong?" he asked. "Something you hated with all your soul? But you couldn't say no because hey! It's family."

"No, actually," Ritchie said. He leaned closer to her to look her in the eye. She folded her arms but stood her ground until he leaned back again.

"No, I don't think you have," he said. "But you know your friend Fitz has. Or should I say *is*."

"I don't know what you're talking about," Ritchie said.

"I know you don't," he said with pity in his voice. "I know. I would never lie to you like that, but he does. You know it actually hurts me? All the things you don't know."

"Not for a minute am I going to entertain the notions you're trying to put into my head," Ritchie said, and tried to stalk off. But she no longer remembered which way was the way back to the dormitories. And Finn, with his long legs, was always going to be able to catch up to her.

"I know. Like I said, I've made my peace with it. You will always put Fitz first," he said.

"It's laughable you even keep putting your two names together like that," Ritchie said, and she could feel the beginnings of anger heating up her blood. "You're nothing to me."

"I know," he said, still too affably. "I can't change that."

"You're right about that," she said, pausing a furious moment to choose between two diverging paths.

"That one will take you back to your building," Finn said, pointing to her left. "I'm going to the right from here. But can I just say one last thing?"

"Can I possibly stop you?"

He laughed again, as if they were engaging in a friendly bout of teasing.

But then his face morphed to something almost sorrowful. "I worry about you. I really do. I swore a promise I cannot break to Fitz to keep his secrets. Despite what you think of me, I'm a man of my word."

Ritchie scoffed, but said nothing.

"So, anyway, when your friend is out in the morning, as I'm sure he will be, maybe you want to have a conversation with him. Clear the air. Bring it all out into the open. It's going to hurt you, I know, and I'm sorry for that. But I think you'll be better for it."

"You think Fitz and I won't be friends again, don't you?" she asked.

"I don't know," he said, and again, he sounded completely honest. "With anyone else, I would say no way. But with you? I don't know what you'll do."

"Well, I can tell you," she said. "I'll be there when Fitz is released, and the two of us will solve this case. If you and your sister had anything to do with it, I swear I'll find a way to prove it. Whatever Fitz is keeping to himself is his business, and it always will be. Now, if you'll excuse me."

She turned away and headed down the path Finn had pointed out to her. It emerged almost at once at a different point on the lawn behind the dormitory building, which was a very good thing.

Blind with rage as she was at the moment, Ritchie would never have found her way back out of that maze before morning.

14

FITZ WOKE to the sounds of voices in his anteroom. He had left the door open the night before, but it was angled such that he couldn't see into it from the bed, and vice versa. Although he was pretty sure someone was keeping an eye on him somehow. He was being detained pending criminal charges, after all.

He was pretty sure he heard Chief Inspector Kasteler's voice, speaking with Blaser, as he pulled his boots on. But then he heard another, more welcome voice.

Colonel Hansen.

He grabbed his tunic and pulled it on as he headed towards the door. Hansen was indeed there, chatting with Blaser as Chief Inspector Kasteler touched a panel out of Fitz's sight, off to one side of his open doorway. There was nothing to see, but something in his ears told him the pressure had just changed.

The force field was down.

"Free to go?" he asked.

"Not exactly," she told him with a tight smile.

"You're being released into my custody," Hansen told him. "They may still charge you with destruction of a crime scene."

"But not murder?" Fitz asked.

"We isolated the poison that was used, as well as the antidote," Kasteler said. "Both were purchased at a specialty apothecary elsewhere on Braga, about four days before you and the rest of the cadets from Oymyakon arrived."

"Do you have a suspect?" Fitz asked.

She gave him an even tighter smile.

"Not for me to know?" he guessed.

"Come with me. We need to process you before you can go," she said, but the hand she put on his shoulder was friendly, almost affectionate.

Blaser gave him the smallest of conspiratorial winks as he went out the door.

Fitz expected another series of events like what he had experienced when he had first been brought in, but apparently the process for leaving was much simpler.

"Cadet Fitz, you are still a person of interest in this case," she told him after she had brought him and Colonel Hansen to her office and closed the door. "You've dropped down on our list of suspects but you haven't been removed from it."

"So you *don't* know who bought the poison and antidote," he guessed. He just couldn't help himself. Hansen gave him a stern look, but Kasteler just carried on as if she hadn't heard him.

"You do not have to stay in visual range of Colonel Hansen at all times, as that would be difficult to arrange when you are auditing classes."

"Oh, good. So I'm still doing that," Fitz said. That earned him a second glare from Hansen.

"You will maintain regular contact with him. If he pings you, you will respond instantly. Is that understood?"

"Yes, chief inspector," Fitz said.

"Your implant is being paroled as well. Do you understand what that means?" she asked him.

"Not exactly," he admitted.

"Your location will be publicly viewable to everyone at all times. Not just the crime investigation unit and the colonel, but everyone."

"Great," he said. He never used his implant's incognito mode, anyway.

"Your implant will also be on a partial lockdown," she went on. "You will still have access to your inbox and calendars and the like, but certain searches will be denied to you. And a search request that triggers a denial will be flagged and brought to my attention."

"What can't I search, exactly?" he asked.

She gave him a wicked sort of grin. "That's the fun part. You won't know until you've triggered it."

"Great," he said, with somewhat less enthusiasm.

It wouldn't matter. If he needed something possibly iffy looked into, he could ask Ritchie or Moreau to do it for him.

Actually, it would have to be Moreau. He had noticed over the last few months that Ritchie never used her implant if she could help it. She spent more time bent over a tablet lately than even Wyss.

"Do I have limitations as to where I can go?" Fitz asked.

"Excellent question. Alas, the answer is it depends," she said.

"Depends on what?" he asked.

"On me," Hansen said. "If you're wanting to go anywhere besides the place you are meant to be according to your daily schedule, you'll clear it with me first."

"Great," Fitz said.

"I don't expect this will be any real inconvenience for you," Kasteler said as she tapped away at her tablet. Then she looked up at him and smiled. "You only have a few days left on Braga, and they will be full of official activities. You aren't even going to have the opportunity for mischief. Not that I think you're planning any. Are you, Cadet Fitz?"

"Not at the moment," he said.

"Then I release you to the responsibility of your commanding officer," she said.

Then she smiled at Colonel Hansen, and it was very different smile than the professional one she'd been blessing Fitz with now and again.

And was that a touch of redness to the colonel's cheeks?

"Come along, cadet," Hansen said, as if anxious to interrupt what he knew Fitz was thinking about.

"Yes, sir," Fitz said, and followed Hansen out the door.

To his surprise, Hansen stopped almost at once, at a food cart at the base of the stairs. He bought two biscuit and egg sandwiches and two coffees.

"You hadn't had breakfast yet," Hansen said as he handed one of the sandwiches to Fitz. Then he bit into his own and chewed with gusto. "I watched Cadet Moreau eat two of these yesterday. They smelled amazing. They don't disappoint."

This last was directed to the vendor, who nodded. "Thank you, sir."

"Grab your coffee, cadet," he said, leading the way across a wide open square. Fitz couldn't jog to catch up, not with a full cup of coffee in his hand, cover or no. But he took longer strides until he was once more by Hansen's side.

"Do they really not have any idea who bought the poison?" he asked around a mouthful of buttery biscuit and piping hot eggs.

"Not yet," Hansen said. "This specialty apothecary is one of those places that doesn't technically break the law, but there are always a ton of irregularities about how they do business. In this case, the owner maintains no security system, which is their right if not a wise decision. They also had a glitch in their invoicing system, where they should have a record of every sale."

"A glitch," Fitz said skeptically.

"Exactly," Hansen said. They had reached the far side of the square and were following a path between two of the large governmental buildings. But once past the buildings, they were back among the ever-present hedges.

"She mentioned a list of suspects, though. They must have something," Fitz said.

Hansen shot him a side-eye. "It's not my case. It's not my jurisdiction. And it's not yours either. Remember, your implant is paroled. Wherever you go, everyone will know, instantly."

"I got that, sir," Fitz said.

"And that includes Ritchie, if you take her with you," Hansen said.

"I gathered that," Fitz said. "I'm not going to drag her into trouble."

"Or vice versa?" Hansen asked.

Fitz laughed. "Yeah, that's probably more likely. But no. I'm not going to risk her career on this, sir."

"And what about your own?" Hansen asked.

"I'm on a list of murder suspects, apparently. Thoughts of my future career are a little lower priority for me at the moment," he said.

"That's probably wise," Hansen said. "Provided you stand back and let the system work."

Fitz was just finishing the last of his coffee when they reached the lawn behind the dormitories. A few cadets were heading towards one of the other paths through the hedges, but they were taking it at a jog and didn't look up as they passed Hansen and Fitz.

"You're meant to be at the diplomat school today," Hansen told him, and irritatingly he pinged Fitz's implant as if he needed to be reminded to check his schedule.

"Got it," Fitz said. "Can I change my uniform first? I've been wearing this since I got here."

"By all means," Hansen said. The corners of his mouth twitched as if he were fighting the urge to smile.

Then they climbed the patio steps to find a single cadet lingering in the breakfast room.

Ritchie.

Hansen chewed at his lip for a moment, then said, "cadets, you're both heading the same way. I'll put you in each other's charge. Ritchie, I'll let them know you're both going to be a little late, as Fitz needs to change into a fresh uniform. But that shouldn't take more than five minutes. I'll be telling them just that."

"Yes, sir," Ritchie said, blinking her eyes in surprise.

"I'm on parole," Fitz explained to her. "My location is being tracked at all times."

"Oh," she said, but like she still didn't completely get it.

Well, he couldn't blame her. He hadn't known what it meant just an hour ago, either.

"Cadets," Hansen said, and ducked out of the room.

Ritchie glanced up at Fitz, then looked away again. "Moreau went with the others up to the school. Colonel Hansen told me to stay back, but not why. I guess I'm happy it's because you're out."

"Yeah. I'm happy about that too," he said. "I should go change, since it sounds like the clock is ticking."

"Sure," she said, stepping aside so she was no longer blocking the door.

Fitz jogged up the stairs to the room he had barely seen and the bed he had never slept in. He opened his bag and shook out a clean, if somewhat wrinkled, uniform. He had showered the day before while in the detention cell. That would have to be good enough; he didn't have time for another one now.

But he did run some water into his hands and scrubbed at his face before finger-combing his hair back into some semblance of order. The one lock that never obeyed his commands immediately fell forward over his forehead, but he let it go, running downstairs to rejoin Ritchie.

Something had changed while he was upstairs. He suspected it was just something in Ritchie's mind, something she was stewing over that she had come to a decision about. But in that moment, it just felt like a storm was about to break out into thunder and lightning right there in the breakfast room.

Was there any way he could run away from this?

Ritchie looked up at him as if determined to speak. Then she flushed and looked down again, as if something had changed her mind.

But then she balled her hands into fists and gave him a more direct look of confrontation.

"Fitz, is there something you're not telling me?" she demanded.

He knew what she meant. There was no doubt in his mind that she was talking about the one thing he had never told her, about what had happened when her father was taken.

He looked her straight in the eyes, trying to guess if either Moreau or Wyss or even Sokolov had let anything spill. He had come clean to two of them the year before, and those two had brought Sokolov in on it for reasons he still didn't understand. But they had all sworn that Fitz should be the one to tell her, not any of them.

Still, Ritchie was perceptive. She had long known that Fitz was hiding something from her. He wouldn't be surprised if she was working out that the other three knew too.

And there was always the far more chilling possibility that Finn had said something to her. He didn't like that thought at all.

But he didn't think she knew, not enough to even guess at what it was she didn't know. Because if she did, he'd see anger there in her eyes. And he didn't.

"About that night? No, I think I told you everything," he said.

A muscle in her jaw tightened. He had just dodged her question, and she was considering whether or not she was going to call him out on that.

"But they do know what poison was used, and where it was acquired," he added.

Ritchie's eyes lit up at that news. She couldn't help herself. He felt a little guilty at how easily he had redirected her. But only a little.

"Really?" she said. "They must be close to catching the killer, then."

"I hope so," he said. "But come on. We're due to audit some diplomat classes, aren't we?"

"Like you have any intention of ever being a diplomat," she said. At first she sounded playful, like old times, two friends teasing each other.

But something caught her up, and he was pretty sure it was the word 'diplomat.'

"Fitz, wait," she said, grabbing his arm when he started to head out to the patio. "We have to talk."

"Now?" he all but wailed. "I'm being monitored, you know. I really can't be late."

"It has to be now, doesn't it?" she said, almost miserably. "It's waited too long. You have to tell me, Fitz. You have to tell me now."

And he could see in her eyes. There would be no running away from it this time.

15

THERE WAS a coppery taste in Ritchie's mouth. She had bitten through her lip again. She hadn't done that in ages. She thought she had broken that habit for good.

But that bad habit wasn't the only thing that kept circling back around again.

As much as she told Finn she wasn't going to let what he was implying get to her, it had. She hadn't slept at all, and had moved numbly through the morning, barely responding to anything Moreau said to her. It was like everything in her existence was on pause, waiting for this moment with Fitz.

She knew she had to be the one to unpause everything. She just couldn't quite make it happen.

Fitz was fuming at her. He didn't want to have this conversation right now. She knew it. He wasn't looking at her, was staring at a point on the floor of the breakfast room with his arms crossed tightly.

He wasn't going to speak first.

A breeze blowing through the room was toying with his hair. Somewhere outside a wind chime was tinkling, drowning out the more distant sound of voices in the gardens. It was a warm breeze, the warmest day so far on Braga, and the floral scent was so heavy on the air it almost gave her a dizzy sort of headache.

"You know I wasn't asking you about that night," she said at last.

He said nothing.

"I saw Finn in the gardens last night," she said.

Now he looked up at her, more alarmed than angry. Although that anger was still there.

"Why?" he asked.

"I was out for a walk and just ran into him," she said. "That's not the important part."

"Come on. You didn't just run into him," he said.

"Obviously," Ritchie said. "He wanted me to know he had nothing to do with what happened to Nils Kaufmann. As if I would take his word for that."

"Well, you took him at his word about something, or you wouldn't be making me late right now," Fitz said.

"I need you to look me in the eye when you tell me what it is you're hiding from me," Ritchie said. He had gone back to staring at that random tile on the floor. She stepped over so that her legs at least were in his view, then waited for him to look up at her.

"I can't do that, Ritchie," he said.

"Because we wouldn't be friends anymore? Are we even friends now?" she asked.

He flinched, but she didn't regret her words. They weren't remotely as harsh as what she was actually feeling.

"My father is gone. Did you know that?" he asked.

Ritchie frowned. "What do you mean, *gone*?"

"Just before the break started, he was given a mission. Top secret. My mother doesn't know where he is or when to expect him back," Fitz said.

"Is that unusual for him?" Ritchie asked, realizing too late she had taken a step closer to him to rest her hand on his arm. The old impulses to be there for him just never went away.

But for once, he didn't pull away from her. He really was upset.

"It's happened before, but never for so long," Fitz said. "We still don't know where he is or when he'll get back."

"Is that why you told Kasteler not to contact him? Because you knew she couldn't?" Ritchie asked.

Fitz looked startled, then laughed. "It didn't even occur to me. Not contacting my parents is sort of my default setting. And anyway, if I need to be bailed out, my mother can handle that as readily as my father. Probably better; she could be here much faster."

"I wouldn't want to cross her," Ritchie said.

Fitz just nodded.

"Well, I'm sorry you don't know where your father is. No one understands better than I do what it's like not knowing if your own father is alive or dead, if he's safe or in pain. I get it. I'm sure it's very stressful for you and your mother. But, Fitz, it's not really relevant to what I just asked you," Ritchie said.

"It is, though," he insisted. "I have to talk to him before I can talk to you. I have to understand some things."

"What kind of things?" she asked.

Fitz took a deep breath. Ritchie sensed he wasn't so much stalling as gathering his thoughts, though, and waited quietly until he was ready to speak. "I've barely spoken to him since you left Buennagel. You know that?"

"You've mentioned it," Ritchie said.

"We were, what, twelve at the time?"

"It was a long time ago."

"Long enough ago that I know when my father told me things, I was getting the for-kids edited version, right?"

"You think he'd be truthful with you now?" Ritchie asked. She was genuinely curious to hear that answer.

"I don't know," Fitz admitted, rubbing at the back of his neck. "I hope so. But it almost isn't even the important thing. I have decisions to make, and I have to know how he answers my questions first. If he feeds me a bunch of lies, well, that's my answer."

"What do you have to decide?" Ritchie asked.

He glanced up at her, just a flash, before looking back down at the floor again. "What I can tell you."

"Why should what your father has to say matter? You don't let what he has to say control anything else about your life," she said.

"That's true," he admitted. "But this is different."

"Because?"

"Because it might not be safe for you to know some things," Fitz said. He took a step back from her, and the hand she had forgotten was resting on his arm slipped away. She could see him shaking, but he wasn't looking at her again.

For her part, she could feel that heartbeat of anger building in her ears. "It's not your job to keep me safe," Ritchie said.

"I'm not protecting you from anything. Not the way you're saying it, anyway," he said. "What I'm doing is not letting my stupid actions put you in danger. And you're not going to change my mind about that."

"How is leaving me in the dark like this, when Finn Berweger clearly knows and is looking to use that knowledge against me in any way keeping me safe?" Ritchie demanded.

"He doesn't know. He just has a guess," Fitz said.

"I'm guessing it's a pretty good guess," Ritchie said.

"Yeah," Fitz had to admit. "Yeah, it's a very good guess. But he doesn't know."

"What happens if your father never comes back?" Ritchie asked, but she forced her voice to soften first. She couldn't ask him that in anger.

"I guess I tell you anyway," Fitz said.

"And how long does he have to be missing before you decide to do that?"

"I don't know," he admitted. "It won't be this week."

"Great," Ritchie said, letting the anger seep back into her voice.

"Maybe it would be better for now if you didn't wander around alone where Finn can corner you?" Fitz suggested.

Ritchie shot him a look of pure fury, to judge from the way he backed away from her. "That's not the answer," she said.

"I just meant for the next few days, until we get off this planet," Fitz said.

Then they both flinched as their respective implants received a high urgency summons from Colonel Hansen. Their lack of movement had finally been noted.

"We have to get going," Fitz said.

"Right," Ritchie agreed, and they headed out of the breakfast room to the patio then down to the lawn.

"Are you really going to audit classes? I didn't think you were even considering the diplomat school," Fitz said as they walked swiftly through the hedges.

"I could say the same thing to you," Ritchie said.

"I signed up to check out both schools. I can't back out of that now, especially when I'm being monitored," he said.

"But you never had any interest in being a diplomat," she said. She heard the edge to her own voice, but she didn't regret it. She was still irritated with him.

All the stress since he had been arrested had only been compounded now that he was out. She had thought she would just be relieved to see him out and the two of them could work the case together, finally.

But now that he was there, she couldn't even focus on it. Her mind couldn't stop turning over what little she knew about what he might be hiding from her. What could possibly interest Finn in any of it?

"I wanted to keep my options open," Fitz said.

"Moreau thinks you're waiting for me to choose first," Ritchie said. She hadn't intended to say that, but now that it was out there, she wasn't going to take it back. "Is that true? What are you waiting for?"

"I'm not waiting," Fitz said. "I'm going to be a guardian. That was always my plan. But it doesn't hurt to be a guardian who understands the diplomat side of things, does it?"

"No," Ritchie agreed. "It's weird. I always knew that after the foreign service academy, the next step was separate schools. But I didn't think it would feel quite so separate as it does."

"They're just a short walk away from each other, but I'm getting the impression that the dinner thing is an unusual exercise in the two schools meeting for any reason," Fitz said.

"You'd think they'd have classes together," Ritchie mused.

"You'd think they'd at least socialize with each other," Fitz said.

"What do you mean?" Ritchie asked. "Surely they hang out on weekends or during breaks?"

"Blaser was guarding my detention room last night, and he's not seen Kung since they got here," Fitz told her. "He sends messages, but Kung barely replies."

"The academic rigor at the diplomat school does seem a little off the charts," Ritchie said. "When Moreau and I were wandering the halls, we stumbled across so many cadets barely holding it together. And one who was outright in tears."

"The guardians take a similar course load," Fitz said. "They must be just as busy. And I'm sure the diplomats hang together to unwind. They just don't do it with the guardians, I guess."

"Aren't you reading a lot into it? I mean, maybe it's just Blaser and Kung."

"You remember them back at the academy. They were tight. Blaser took punishment for not revealing Kung's location because he knew Kung needed a break. Remember?"

Ritchie frowned. She did remember how tight they were. All the way up until the moment they stepped on the intergalactic railway together at the end of their final semester, they had been nearly inseparable.

"It does sound odd," she admitted. But they had reached the steps up to the entrance of the diplomat school. "Maybe we'll learn something useful today."

"About diplomacy or about the case?" Fitz asked her in something close to his old teasing tone.

"I hope both," she said. "My schedule says I'm due for a class in emotional control. And doesn't *that* sound like tons of fun."

"I'm heading to the same class," Fitz said. "Let's do this."

They jogged up the steps, back into the cold halls that echoed with nearly inaudible whispers. It didn't feel like emotional control was anything these cadets needed to take a class in. The entire building was demanding it of them just by its entire oppressive feel.

And yet even as they moved through halls empty of cadets because classes were already in session, somewhere softly she could hear someone breathing their way to enforced calmness and not tears. Were they using the lessons they had learned to do that? And not quite succeeding?

One way or the other, this was going to be a very interesting class.

16

THE CLASS WAS ALREADY in session when they arrived, but that wasn't as disruptive as Fitz had feared. The open floor plan allowed the garden breezes to flow in through the open French doors onto a patio on the far end of the room and then continue flowing into the hallway through the tangle of viney plants that was as close as the room got to a wall.

It was just as easy for a pair of cadets to flow in the other way and linger at the back of the room between garden and corridor and get a sense of things before the instructor even noticed they were there.

If there had been any sort of lecture happening, it had just ended. The diplomat cadets were milling around the space, forming up into groups of two or four. Moreau was already waving for Ritchie to join her and two diplomat cadets at the far side of the room.

"Go on," Fitz said to her. "I'll find a place."

"Sure," Ritchie said, not exactly giving him a second look before rushing over to join her buddy.

She was calmer now than she had been, but she was still carrying a little anger against him. Well, that was okay. He deserved it.

"Are you in this class or just watching?" someone asked him. He turned to see an older student in a diplomat cadet uniform smiling at him with her hands folded together over her stomach as she waited for his answer.

"I'm auditing," he said. "Cadet Fitz."

"I'm Diplomat Cadet Veronika Hefti," she said, then extended her hand to give him a very correct handshake. "I'm a last-year student here, but I assist the instructor with this class. I believe everyone else is already paired off, but I can work with you if you like."

He looked her over. She did look slightly older than the other cadets in the room. But more than that, she looked far more exhausted. Her pale face was thin in an unhealthy way, to the point where her cheeks were grayish hollows and her dark blue eyes looked too big on her face. But her uniform was like her handshake, perfectly correct in every detail. Her hair was pulled back in a braided bun that looked like it scored high on the difficulty scale, but didn't give off an elaborate-for-show vibe. It spoke more of competence in all things than any sort of fashion sense.

"That sounds good to me," Fitz said to her. "I suppose you assist in this class because you excel at the subject matter?"

"I did score very highly," she said, and the gray of her cheeks turned ever so slightly pink.

"My schedule just said the class is called 'emotion control', but it didn't exactly define that," Fitz said as Hefti led him to two free chairs on the side of the room closest to the garden. The floral scent was stronger here, but the breeze was also warmer than deeper within the marble building.

"What's your question?" she asked as they sat down.

"I guess, controlling your emotions sounds like an area of study that's going to take more than one semester," he said.

"Two things," she said, and held up a finger. "Firstly, it *is* a big topic, and in a lot of ways it lasts not just throughout your four years here at this school but throughout your entire life as a diplomat and, I'm sure, beyond."

"Sure," Fitz agreed amiably.

"And second," she went on, holding up two fingers. "We don't really learn how to control our emotions here. The important thing as a diplomat is to control the expression of your emotions."

"Keep it close to the chest, right," Fitz said, nodding.

She frowned at him. "It's not about hiding facts from others. There are several species that the Union of Free Worlds negotiates with on an ongoing basis who find the human expression of emotion distasteful or distracting or even outright upsetting."

"So controlling it is just good manners," Fitz said, just going along with whatever she wanted to say. It felt like the diplomatic thing to do.

"There are species who express anger by releasing a gas which is toxic to humans," Hefti told him sternly. "Many diplomats have been injured in such cases. And we have done the same or similar things to others. It is important to learn control."

"Of course," Fitz said. "So, what's the key? Holding your breath and counting to ten?"

"Holding your breath is not as effective as slowing down your breath and focusing on it. Control your breath, and you are already well on your way to controlling a lot of other things about your body," she said.

"Slow breath in, slow breath out?" Fitz said, and demonstrated what he thought she meant.

"Good, but even slower if you can," she said, and started taking slow breaths herself. "Normally I don't do this so loudly it could be heard."

"Sure. But for demonstration purposes," Fitz said, still breathing slowly.

"Very good," she said. "Now, close your eyes. Try to keep your breathing exactly as it is now, slow and even, and in sync with your own rhythm."

Fitz closed his eyes, let his hands rest half-open on his knees, and just enjoyed breathing in the warm garden-fresh air.

He felt a tickle on the back of his neck before he even realized that Hefti had gotten up from her chair. But he ignored it, focusing on his breathing, just as she had told him to do.

She tickled at his nose, almost to the point where he felt like he had to sneeze, but he fought back the urge and just kept breathing.

Something hot was pressed to his hand, but he didn't react. Then there was a truly foul odor just under his nose. That was the hardest, and he tried switching to breathing through his mouth. But that just made the stink coat the back of his throat and it was like he was drinking down hot, vile garbage juice.

He was pretty sure he was visibly reacting to that, but only subtly. He didn't flinch away.

"You can open your eyes now, Cadet Fitz," Hefti said as she sat back down in her chair. He opened his eyes and looked around for the source of the smell, but it was gone now. "Have you had training before?"

"Just my whole life growing up in a military household," Fitz said. His tone was joking, but he was half serious.

"Yes, I suppose," Hefti said thoughtfully. "And you're looking to come to the diplomat school? That is interesting."

"No, I'm really not," he confessed. "But I do find the training you do here interesting. This class in particular. Being able to control your outward responses to things must really come in handy sometimes, right?"

"Some of us use it more than others," she said, glancing around the room behind him. He was tempted to turn and figure out who she was singling out as the less-thans, but he stayed where he was, watching her face.

"I suppose it's good everyone gets this class in the first semester. I understand it's the toughest time," he said.

She gave him a look that mixed surprise, amusement, and just a touch of disdain. "Whoever told you that?"

He cast his mind back, but all he could come up with was, "everyone?"

"Everyone at the guardian school, I'm sure," she said with a dismissive wave.

"That's not true here?" he asked.

"The first semester is tough. So is the second, the third, and all the others that follow. Things here are constantly building up from what you've learned before. It never gets easier," she said with a sniff.

"I'm sure the guardians feel the same way about their curriculum," Fitz said. "I think they were just trying to buck up our spirits."

"Hm," Hefti said, as if she didn't approve of such impulses.

"It feels very intense, the environment in this school," Fitz said.

"You know only a third of foreign service academy cadets choose to come here?" she asked.

Fitz nodded.

"We're the top third. Maybe not by foreign service academy grading standards. But if you thin out the grades based on… other competencies, you'll find the top third of the most academically driven cadets all come here," she said.

"It sounds like a lot of pressure," Fitz said.

"We can handle it," she assured him.

"I believe it," he said. "You know, the first day here, I was sitting with Nils Kaufmann at the gala dinner thing."

He wasn't done talking, but he faltered a moment in his words. Something subtle had just shifted on her face. She was still looking at him with keen interest in her dark blue eyes, and her posture was all attentive listening. But something in her face had hardened, ever so slightly.

He had just seen her drop a mask over her face. She really was studied with controlling the external manifestation of her emotions.

Now he just *had* to test her.

"I'm sorry. I didn't mean to bring up the tragedy," he said. "I know he was well-loved."

"Yes, Kaufmann was a diplomat cadet worthy of every admiration," she said dryly. "But that's not what you were going to say?"

"No, I was about to say, I got to talk with him a little before that all happened," Fitz said. He was only half intentionally making a mess of getting the words out. But her face remained implacable. Not cold or wooden. She still gave every indication of being an attentive listener. It was just he knew that was a lie. She was hiding something.

"He was a last-year student, right? Top of the class? And he seemed quite cool with all of it. Not stressed at all," Fitz said. "Was that an act? Or was he just so brilliant nothing here was a challenge?"

She blinked. He was sure that meant something. He just didn't know what. Had she been crushing on Nils? Was she hiding her broken heart from his, admittedly, prying eyes?

Well, he knew one way to find out.

"I have a close friend who started here this semester. Feena Berweger. Do you know her?" he asked, and just resisted the temptation to bat his eyes in a show of innocence. It was a good bet that Hefti was as good at reading other people as she was with hiding her own tells. She surely already guessed he was up to something here. No need to lay it on thick.

"Feena Berweger? Tall blonde? Sure, I think we've all noticed her," she said. Her words had just a hint of coolness to them, letting Fitz know that as much as she wasn't going to say so out loud, she really didn't care for Feena Berweger.

But was that emotional tell slipping out by accident, because her emotions were just so strong?

No, Fitz guessed she was letting it out because as much as she really didn't like Feena, she felt less need to keep that secret than whatever she had felt about Kaufmann.

Fitz sat forward in his chair, anxious to ask another question and gauge her response, but the instructor he had never actually paid any attention to was clapping his hands at the other end of the classroom.

Fitz had never been more disappointed at the end of a class. Especially one that ended with lunch.

"Well, I'm sorry to hear you've already set your heart on the guardian school, but I hope you enjoy the rest of your day here at our school," Hefti said to him, reaching out to shake his hand one last time.

"Thank you for a very interesting class," he said to her with complete sincerity.

Perhaps too much sincerity, to judge by the eyebrow Moreau was cocking up at him as she and Ritchie approached.

"Hello. Diplomat Cadet Hefti, right?" Ritchie said to Hefti. Hefti, who had been shoving a tablet into her bag, looked up and gave Ritchie a generic smile that only turned a shade more genuine when she placed her.

"Ritchie? And… I'm sorry, I forgot your name," she said to Moreau. "I hope you're enjoying your day here at the school. I'd love to chat with you some more, but I have another class to get to and it's on the other side of the building, so you really must excuse me."

"Sure," Ritchie said to Hefti's rapidly departing back.

"You know Hefti already?" Fitz asked as he got up from the chair and stretched the kinks out of his back.

"Yeah," Ritchie said. "She was the cadet I told you about before. The one Moreau and I found crying in the hallway."

"Her?" Fitz said in disbelief. She had seemed so in control to him. And not remotely stressed out by anything.

He supposed anyone could have a bad day, though.

He followed Ritchie and Moreau to the cafeteria for lunch with the other cadets. But he wished Hefti hadn't run away so hastily. He really wanted to keep asking her questions. Her muted responses were just so fascinating.

17

RITCHIE WASN'T sure what she had assumed the diplomat school cafeteria was going to look like. Something cold and formal, like the school itself.

Or, frankly, like the two food settings she had already experienced at the school, if out on the patio.

But this wasn't a meet and greet event, and it definitely wasn't a learning experience in navigating unfamiliar protocols.

It was just the daily grind of cadets taking a refueling break in the middle of a long, exhausting day.

It was actually really nice. Warm and welcoming.

The room itself was cozy by diplomat school standards. It was built on a lower level with no garden access, although a row of windows high along the walls provided ample sunlight. But those windows were all sealed glass, no cool breeze and no floral scents were wafting across the dining area. Just the warmth of the kitchens and the smell of the food.

Which today was fish and chips. The chips weren't made from potatoes, but something equally starchy, if with a bit of a sweeter taste. And it was all served fresh from the fryer and piping hot.

Ritchie, Fitz and Moreau piled up platefuls of the stuff, along with sides of some sort of creamy salad with both shredded cabbage and cubes of a golden fruit as its base. Then they found a table near the center of the room and sat down together.

Something, Ritchie realized with a pang, they barely ever did back on Oymyakon anymore. Indeed, Fitz seemed positively giddy after their class. Which seemed really odd to Ritchie. She had found the subject matter baseline dry, bordering on creepy.

"So they let you out?" Moreau said to him as she stirred her salad around with her fork.

"They paroled my implant," Fitz said smugly.

"You say that like it was on your bucket list or something," Moreau smirked at him.

"Well, it would've been if I had known it was a thing," he said. "It just means they can follow me everywhere I go and know whatever I use the implant for."

"Like what?" Moreau asked around a mouthful of salad.

"So far? Checking my schedule so I can get to class," he said. "Theoretically? I guess they think I might be inclined to use it to research how to get away with murder."

"Hush!" Ritchie said. "It's not a joking matter. They could put you back in detention at any time. They don't even need much of a reason."

"No, Fitz's general attitude is probably enough," Moreau agreed.

"I'm behaving," he insisted.

For a moment, they all turned their attention to the food, plowing through the golden mounds of fish before they got cold. But the chips were excellent at resisting the inevitable transition into soggy lumps, and Fitz munched at one while looking around the cafeteria.

"See anyone we know?" Ritchie asked, scanning the tables she could see behind him. The cadets looked much more relaxed here. A few were bent over tablets, studying while they ate, but no one looked as close to burn-out as the cadets she had seen in the halls.

Was that because the burning out cadets didn't make time for lunch? Or was something in the hallways just messing with everyone's heads?

"A few cadets from Oymyakon," Fitz said with a shrug. "But mainly I was trying to guess who around us might be a killer."

"Fitz!" Ritchie admonished him again.

But now Moreau was scanning the room. "Considering what we learned today, I think we'd have to admit it could be any one of them."

"Nothing we learned today turns people into murderers," Ritchie said.

"No, just that, if they all learn how to hide their emotions like that, it could be anyone and we wouldn't be able to tell," Moreau said.

"Hey, guys!" Heim said as she approached their table with a tray in her hands. "Can I sit with you for a bit?"

"Sure, plenty of room," Fitz said, and he and Moreau slid their chairs closer to Ritchie so that Heim could squeeze in between them.

"Thanks," she said. "I'm running late, but I'm also starving." She shoved an entire piece of fish in her mouth and munched away, then swallowed before asking, "what classes did you guys audit this morning?"

"We were all in the same one. Emotion control," Ritchie said.

"Right, I should've guessed," Heim said as she salted her chips. "They start everyone with that. If that class creeps you out, you're definitely not going to make it as a diplomat."

"I guess that's me out then," Ritchie admitted.

Moreau gave her a look of surprise. "Seriously?"

"You didn't find that creepy?" Ritchie asked.

"I would've thought you would find it beneath your level," Fitz said blandly as he stirred around the remaining crumbs on his plate.

"The cadets working with us did say she was a natural," Ritchie told him.

"Ha ha," Moreau said sarcastically. "But I did find it interesting. It could be helpful in all kinds of situations. The kind of situations that spring out on you out of nowhere, catching you all unaware. Practicing those techniques is really good self-defense."

"I agree," Heim said around a mouthful of food.

"I found it interesting as well," Fitz said.

"You seemed very interested," Ritchie said.

"I think that Diplomat Cadet Hefti had feelings for Kaufmann," Fitz said.

"Really?" Ritchie said, and looked to Moreau.

"When we saw her crying, he wasn't dead yet," Moreau said. "But I suppose it's possible she was crying because he had spurned her or something?"

"No," Ritchie said after mulling it over for a moment. "I don't think so. That wasn't broken heart crying, that was stressed out crying."

"No reason why she couldn't be both incredibly stressed out when you saw her crying and upset now because of Kaufmann," Fitz said.

"She didn't seem upset," Ritchie said. "In a hurry, but not emotional."

"That's just what I'm saying," Fitz insisted. "She was hiding something from me. I could tell."

"After just one class?" Ritchie said skeptically.

"Whatever, Ritchie," he said, as if exhausted with talking to her.

"Does this mean you're changing your mind about which school you want to go to?"

"Not remotely," he said, but then turned to Heim. "I did want to ask you something, though."

"We wanted to ask," Ritchie corrected him.

He ignored her. "There are a lot of Oymyakon cadets in the first year here. There are even more at the guardian school. You guys were all friends last year. Why are you so cold to each other now?"

"Cold?" Heim said, as if she wasn't sure what the word meant. "I don't think we're cold. Busy, maybe."

"Too busy to ever relax a little?" Fitz asked.

Ritchie shot him a look, begging him to back off with the aggressive tone. But Heim didn't seem bothered. She just shrugged. "I don't think anyone here is ignoring anyone at the guardian school just because we're in different schools now. It's not cliquey or anything. It's just that being in diplomat school keeps us very, very busy."

"The guardians have a similar course load," Ritchie said. "Everyone takes the same number of classes for the same hours of the day."

"True," Heim said slowly, "but their classes are very different from ours."

"Different how?" Ritchie pressed.

"A lot of their training is physical," Heim said. "We have to take a physical training credit every semester too, but they do a lot more."

"It sounds exhausting," Moreau said.

Heim smiled at her. "I know, right? But no homework. And guardians have a lot more practical classes, workshops and things. Again, not much homework. Whereas here, we have classes that are 10% lecture and 90% outside reading and papers and other projects. So, like I said, we're all quite busy."

"Clearly, I've made the right choice, then," Fitz said with audible relief.

Ritchie just stared down at the plate in front of her. She knew she shouldn't say so out loud, but she liked homework. She liked tackling a reading assignment on her own and then supplementing or redirecting that knowledge with a lecture from an instructor. She liked forming her own ideas and articulating them into a paper.

She just really liked homework.

Moreau was asking Heim about something, but the sound was just a low drone in Ritchie's ears.

Then Fitz leaned over and said, "you know, there's no rule that says guardian cadets can't do as much extra reading as they like outside of class, right?"

Ritchie looked up at him in surprise. He was just cocking an eyebrow at her as he ate the last of his fries, a crispy bit that was more oil than vegetable.

As usual, he had known exactly what she was thinking.

"What classes do you have now?" Heim asked as she started stacking her dishes neatly on her tray.

"Military protocols," Fitz said with a grimace. "I didn't pick it."

"No, they pick the classes for us," Ritchie said, then accessed her implant to check her own schedule. "Social stratification in various union and nonunion societies." It sounded like a big topic she wasn't going to get much of a takeaway from after a single class. But she was just there to get a feel for things, right?

"Interplanetary trade agreements," Moreau said, and she sounded as excited as Ritchie had ever heard her.

"With Professor Foster?" Heim asked. Moreau nodded. "That's on the other side of the school from here. I'm heading that way, but we'd have to go now to get there in time."

"See you," Moreau said to Ritchie and Fitz, and ran to join Heim at the tray return area.

"I think this all just got a lot more complicated," Ritchie said with a sigh.

"What's that?" Fitz asked. "Deciding on what school?"

"No, solving this case," Ritchie said. "I still have no leads at all."

"Well, we have been tied up with other things," Fitz reminded her. Then his eyes unfocused, and she knew he was reading a somewhat lengthy message on his implant.

"What is it?" she asked.

"I just got a message from Blaser at the guardian school. And someone called Zahnd. Another guardian cadet, I think," he said slowly as he scanned whatever his implant was projecting in his field of vision.

"I know her," Ritchie said. "What do they want?"

"They want to talk to us. About the case," Fitz said.

"Well, obviously, we can't do that now," Ritchie said.

"Actually, we can," Fitz said with a sheepish grin. Before she could even ask what he meant, her implant pinged. Her schedule had been updated. She was now due at the guardian school.

"What's going on?" she asked, narrowing her eyes at him.

"You need to make a decision," Fitz said. "If you really want to be a diplomat, you should probably go find that class you're meant to be in. Society blah blah blah."

"While you do what?"

"While I go see Blaser and Zahnd and whoever else they have with them about what happened at that dinner party," he said. "We were in the middle of a case, you know."

"I know what I've been doing, as useless as it was," Ritchie said. "But you were cooling your heels in detention up until an hour ago."

"You think I didn't find a way to work from there? How do you think Blaser even knew to get in touch with me?" he asked her.

"This is seriously about solving the murder? Because Hansen told me to stay out of it. And you are being watched all the time," Ritchie said.

"I admit that makes things a little more uncomfortable, but we can manage. This schedule change is completely on the up and up. Perfectly official, through all the correct channels. I'll be doing what I'm supposed to be doing. And if you come with me, so will you."

Ritchie gave him a skeptical look.

"Unless you're serious about the diplomat thing. Skipping the auditing might not remove you from contention, but it will be a black mark against you. And you probably want to see what the other classes are like. It's up to you," Fitz said.

"Have you considered the possibility that Kaufmann was killed by mistake? That *you* were the target?" Ritchie asked him.

"The thought has crossed my mind," he admitted.

She leaned in closer to him, letting the hubbub of the cafeteria around them cover up her words as she asked, "is it part of everything else? Your father and your secret and everything?"

"I certainly hope not," he said, but too quickly. She kept up her most skeptical look, not wavering until he had considered his answer more carefully. "I don't think so. But it's a possibility. And if it *is* connected, it's definitely something the crime investigation unit is not considering. Like the Berwegers, whom you and I must agree should be suspects."

Ritchie half shrugged and half nodded.

"Hence this meeting," Fitz said. "But I can do this without you and catch you up later if you need to get to those classes."

Ritchie bit down on her already sore lip. She was supposed to have a few more days and a lot more information about her options before she made this decision.

But she realized she didn't need any of those things. She really had already decided.

"Let's go," she said, pushing up from the table.

Fitz stood up as well. Even as he gathered up the trash from their table, she could see him fighting the urge to grin at her.

If he thought this felt like old times, she would have to agree. The problem was, she knew that was just temporary. Did he?

"We're still not friends," she warned him. "We can't be until you clear the air between us."

"I know," he said. "But for now, we're colleagues, right? Working together to find out just what happened to Nils Kaufmann and catch the guilty parties?"

"Colleagues," Ritchie agreed.

It was actually a relief, having something else to focus on. She hated thinking about what divided her from Fitz. Working together might be just pretending that they were still friends, but it was a nice break from not being friends.

She couldn't pretend forever, but she could manage it for a few days.

18

THE MESSAGE from Blaser had come with directions to meet at the back of the guardian school, where they had attended the first of the first day's three parties. Fitz wasn't sure who would be meeting them in the middle of the day, who was willing to skip classes to work on a clandestine investigation. There were a lot of consequences to those actions, and no guarantee that even if they solved the case, the risks would be worth it.

Fitz sneaked a glance over at Ritchie. She had calmed down, but he could see her anger still simmering just under the surface. He should probably get used to that. He doubted it would go away before he came clean to her.

But the niggling worry that maybe, just maybe, Kaufmann had been killed when he, Shackleton Fitz IV, was the real target only made him more determined to talk to his father first.

He knew his family wasn't as prominent or as powerful as the Berwegers, but they were pretty close. And not having spoken to his father for so many years, he had put himself at a real disadvantage at understanding the risks he might face just living as a Fitz.

He hadn't managed to get the words out, but when his mother had told him that his father was on a secret mission and couldn't be reached, he had instantly wondered whether his father was dead already.

If someone else in the military had wanted to get rid of him, a secret mission that rendered him unreachable was the perfect cover, wasn't it? It would be a long, long time before anyone else started to wonder if something had happened to him.

In the meantime, Fitz's mother was running the family. But maybe it should be him. Maybe looking at schools was an exercise in futility. If his father never came back, his future had already been chosen for him. Quite aside from his father's military career, just managing their estate on Buennagel was a full-time occupation.

He didn't know what was going on with his father or any of the rest of it. It would be pretty ironic if he were killed as part of some political machination he didn't even understand.

But if Nils Kaufmann had been killed in his place, that would just be tragic.

Fitz really hoped that wasn't what had happened.

Finally, they emerged from the humid warmth of the hedge maze to the wide expanse of lawn that ran up to the patio at the back of the guardian school. Blaser was there waiting for them, standing beside a long table with a half a dozen chairs around it. Fitz recognized the blond woman standing beside him as someone who had spoken to Ritchie at that first party. Zahnd, he assumed.

And already seated at the table were Bale and Egli.

Who were willing to skip class and face the consequences of that? Only the top guardian cadets. He couldn't suppress the grin that spread across his face.

"Ritchie! I hoped you'd come," Zahnd said as she saw the two of them coming up the steps.

"Aren't you worried about getting into trouble?" Ritchie asked. "You work for Kasteler. This can't have been an easy choice for you."

"Oh, I'm not here," she said with a wink.

"You didn't strike me as a rule-breaker," Ritchie said, but Zahnd just grinned at her.

"Everyone here was at the dinner in question," Blaser said. "Well, not me, but I organized this meeting."

"This isn't every guardian at the dinner," Fitz noted.

"No, but we can get in touch with the others," Bale said. "We'll answer your questions as well as we can. We already asked the others everything we could think of. But if you need to know more, we'll network with the others to see if we can find you better answers."

"We have to keep it on the down low, though," Egli said. "We're not allowed to interfere in active investigations."

"But you're willing to this time," Fitz said. "Just for curiosity's sake, why?"

The three former Oymyakon cadets exchanged a glance, then said as one, "the Berwegers."

"You two were gone before they arrived," Fitz pointed out.

"We have an informal group of former Oymyakon cadets," Bale said. "Just a casual meetup now and then of everyone in all years here who came out of that academy."

"So you heard of the Berwegers through them?" Fitz guessed.

"We heard stories from last year's crop," Egli said. "I admit, I thought they were exaggerating. Then this year started and the Berwegers themselves arrived."

"Plus those of us who knew them best, for as much as that's worth," Blaser said. "We've done our best to keep an eye on them."

"It would be easier if we had diplomat cadets working with us," Bale said.

"For now, we're just focusing on the events of this dinner," Zahnd said. "For my part, I was working with the crime investigation unit that night. I didn't arrive until after everything had gone down. I can tell you that no evidence collected by us has any link to the Berwegers."

"So you know who bought the poison and antidote?" Fitz asked.

"No, that's still a mystery," Zahnd said. "But I checked some records myself after talking to Blaser here. The Berwegers have a private shuttle they keep here for their own use. It hasn't moved since they arrived weeks ago. If they traveled to the far side of the planet, they didn't use their own vehicle to do it."

"But anyone could use public transport," Blaser said, and Fitz could tell they were rehashing for him and Ritchie an argument the two of them had already had between themselves.

"Would they do that, though?" Ritchie asked.

"If they did, they'd be on record," Fitz said. "The apothecary might not keep a security video feed, but that can't be true of every station between here and there, surely."

"No, they aren't on any of the recordings. I checked that too," Zahnd said.

"That still doesn't rule them out," Ritchie sighed. "Anyone could have gone to make that purchase for them. Another diplomat cadet, a random gardener, anyone at all."

"That is the problem," Bale agreed, nodding.

"Bale, you and Egli were at the tables pretending to be the visiting species, correct?" Fitz asked.

"Yes, I was about four tables away from you, and Egli was at the far end of the patio," he said.

"Practically as far as you could get from the head table without being on the lawn," Egli said. "It gave me a very expansive view of everything."

"Were you paying close attention?" Ritchie asked. "I mean, it was meant to be a party."

"Well, like we just said, we've all been kind of hyperaware of the Berwegers since they arrived," she said. "So I was watching them while they worked the tables. That was pretty easy for me to do with Finn. He was at my end of things."

"Far from me," Fitz said, and she nodded.

"Feena followed you to your table, but then she went back to her own section, closer to the head table. She never went back to your area again," Bale said.

"But we never really thought they'd done anything directly themselves," Ritchie pointed out.

"They didn't have any interactions with the other servers that I noticed," Egli said, and Bale nodded in agreement.

"Again, why would they act openly, though?" Fitz said. "They must have arranged everything beforehand."

"If they were involved at all," Zahnd said.

"It would be impossible to rule out, wouldn't it?" Fitz mused. "Especially if another diplomat cadet turns out to be the culprit. I'm sure since arriving at the school, the Berwegers have had at least one point of contact with everyone there."

"We need eyes on the inside," Blaser grumbled to himself.

"We need to accept we're not likely to pin this on them even if they are ultimately responsible," Ritchie said with a sigh. "We have to find whoever actually did the deed. We can hope that leads back to them, but maybe it doesn't."

"Maybe they didn't do it," Zahnd said.

"Are you here just to take their part?" Fitz asked, annoyed.

"I'm not here at all," she said.

"I get you mean that we should deny you were here if asked, but come on," Fitz said.

"Fitz," Ritchie said warningly.

"No, it's all right," Zahnd said. "You are correct, officially I'm not here, but physically I am. You can check your implant now if you like. I'm not here. And yet I am."

"And your point is?" Fitz asked.

"I'm here for the sake of fairness and justice," Zahnd said. "It would be terribly ironic if all of you in the fight against conspiracies which are driving events from under the surface should start behaving the same way as those you're hunting down."

Fitz glowered at her, but Ritchie put her hand on his arm again, just where she had before when he had told her about his father. It was more the memory than the gesture that distracted him.

"She's right, Fitz," Ritchie said. "We can't fight a conspiracy by starting a conspiracy of our own."

Fitz barked out a laugh. "And Hansen's task force is what now?"

"Officially sanctioned," Ritchie said confidently.

"By whom?" he asked her.

She faltered at that.

"I'm not saying you aren't both right about the danger these siblings represent," Zahnd said blandly. "I'm just saying, you don't have proof. And without proof, you don't have anything at all. Just whispered accusations."

"Seriously?" Bale asked her. "How many cadets have to whisper what their guts are telling them before the higher ups take it seriously? We can't all be wrong."

"Of course you can," Zahnd said. "Groups of people gather around bad ideas all the time."

Egli and Blaser both reddened with anger, and Blaser looked like he was about to start really arguing with Zahnd, but Fitz put up a hand to belay him.

"She's entitled to her opinion, guys," he said.

"Her opinion stinks," Blaser spat out.

"I don't disagree," Fitz said.

"You can't condemn people without trial or even evidence," Zahnd said. "That's not how we do things here."

"On Braga?" Blaser asked her.

She blinked at him in surprise. "In the Union of Free Worlds, cadet."

"Look, for now, let's just gather what evidence we can, right?" Ritchie said. "If it points to the Berwegers or not, that's something we deal with after we have that evidence. Right?"

"Who we think is guilty is guiding where we look for evidence, isn't it?" Fitz asked.

Ritchie opened then closed her mouth to think more before she spoke. Then she turned to Zahnd. "How far can we push things before someone gets upset? I know we can't break into the crime investigation unit's computer systems to examine the physical evidence ourselves, for instance. But how much can we talk to cadets before it crosses a line?"

Zahnd rubbed at her chin as she pondered the question. "That would really depend on whether or not any cadets complain about you asking questions."

"Is anyone likely to complain?" Ritchie asked.

"Sure, the guilty parties," Fitz said. "If we get a reaction to questions, we're going to have to act fast from there."

"If you really don't think anything happened during the meal itself, there's not much we guardian cadets can do to help you," Bale said.

"Sadly, I agree. But thanks for the offer of help," Fitz said.

"We should get back to class, then," Egli said, and she and Bale headed back into the building.

"I have to get back to the crime investigation building," Zahnd said. "I still hope to see you later this week, Ritchie."

"Yeah, me too," Ritchie said, but she sounded distracted as she watched Zahnd walk away.

"Rack time for me," Blaser said.

"I imagine so. You were on duty all night," Fitz said. "Thanks for arranging this."

"As much use as it was," Blaser said glumly.

"Every bit helps," Fitz assured him. "Keep working on Kung, though. If I've learned anything from this trip to Braga, it's that the guardian cadets and the diplomat cadets are operating at too much distance from each other."

"Will do," Blaser said, then headed into the building to find his bunk.

And so Fitz found himself once more alone with Ritchie. "Do you want to head back to the diplomat school?"

"I suppose so," she said. Then she sighed. "We should've stayed with our original schedule."

He didn't answer her. He wasn't sure what he had hoped for with this meeting, but it certainly didn't seem to have accomplished anything much.

Well, it had introduced him to Zahnd, who really irritated him. But she and Ritchie seemed like friends already.

In the end, it didn't matter which schools either of them chose. There was going to be a distance between them, even when they stood within arm's reach of each other.

"Let's go," Fitz said, and headed back into the hedges.

19

RITCHIE HAD THOUGHT that Fitz was leading them back to the diplomat school, but after twice the usual time had passed, she realized she had no idea where they were. The sun directly overhead was almost too hot now that they had no shade. And there was no sound of other cadets anywhere around them. In fact, she was pretty sure the buzz she heard was from bees. A lot of bees, somewhere not too far away.

"Where are we going?" she finally asked Fitz.

He looked up, startled. And she realized he hadn't been leading them anywhere. He had just been walking.

"Do you know where we are?" he asked her sheepishly.

"No," she said, annoyed with him all over again. "Does anyone know where this place is? It doesn't look like even the gardeners come out here." Indeed, the flowerbeds that ran alongside the path were filled with the bedraggled remains of flowers losing the war with brightly green weeds.

"Maybe this is good," Fitz said. "No one is out here. We can talk without being overheard."

"We're not where you're supposed to be, remember?" Ritchie said.

"I'll tell them I got lost," he said. "Let's keep moving, but slowly, like we're looking for the way back."

"Fine," she said, but had no idea which way to start the pantomime. Fitz nodded his head in the direction they had already been heading, and she followed along.

"Do you really agree with Zahnd that the Berwegers are innocent?" he asked.

That question threw her for a loop. "Are you serious?"

"You said you agreed with her," he said.

"I agreed that we have to be careful not to fight fire with fire here," she said. "Don't you agree with that? What good does it do to uncover a conspiracy if it means creating a conspiracy of our own to do it? That's still not society functioning the way it's supposed to."

Fitz grinned at her. "That's the most diplomat thing I've ever heard you say."

"Guardians uphold the social order," she shot back. He shrugged, but the grin didn't fade.

"I don't know if the Berwegers are innocent or not in this," Ritchie said. "Like I *did* say in the meeting, we have to let the evidence guide us, don't we?"

"Sure," Fitz said with another shrug.

"Why did you ask, then?"

"Well, you said that Finn was alone with you last night," Fitz said.

"So?"

"Well," he drawled. She stopped walking to glare at him until he finally spit out the rest of his sentence. "If he put a whammy on you, you might be on his side now."

"You know that's not how it works," Ritchie said. "We've never seen anyone who got hit harder than Moreau, and she never changed sides."

"That's true," Fitz said, but there was still a drawl to his words.

"You think she's better able to fight off their influence than I am?" Ritchie asked. Her hands curled into fists. A part of her was totally prepared to slug him if she didn't like his answer.

"No, I wouldn't say that," he said. Still so slowly.

"What would you say, Fitz?"

"I think Finn has probably gained skill since then," Fitz said.

"That's not all you're thinking," she guessed.

"I think he wants you more," Fitz said. Ritchie felt her cheeks flush, and he waved his hands hastily as if trying to dispel her thoughts. "He wants you on his side more. We're long past the days when he and his sister didn't see fit to invite you to their little conspiracy parties. He knows you too well now. He wants you and your skills for something."

Ritchie bit back her anger until she was done thinking those words through. Then it just faded away to calmness. "I think you're probably right," she agreed. "He watches me a lot. I don't like it."

"I'm glad to hear it," Fitz said. "That you don't like it, I mean. I'd prefer he weren't constantly creeping you out."

"I know what you meant," Ritchie said.

They walked in silence for a few more turnings of the path, but something was clearly still on Fitz's mind. Finally he asked, "so you *don't* think he's innocent, then?"

"I saw him burn a body," Ritchie reminded him. "He says his parents coerced him into it, but I don't care whether that's true or not. He's responsible for his own actions in the end, and I saw him destroy evidence."

"Good," Fitz said, but after another awkwardly long pause he continued, "so Finn finding you alone in the gardens at night was just a professing his innocence thing?"

Ritchie grabbed his arm to drag him to a stop. "What are you accusing me of?" she demanded.

"Me? Nothing," he said. "I don't exactly relish the idea of him being alone with you. I know what he's capable of. I'd prefer if you'd stick with Moreau if you won't stick with me."

"I can handle myself," Ritchie said.

"With anybody else, I would wholeheartedly agree," he said.

They stood there for a long moment, the bees buzzing all around them if nowhere actually in sight. This time, he didn't drop his eyes. She held his gaze, searching his eyes for clues. In the end, she was sure it was merely concern, not jealousy, that was driving his words.

But for reasons she didn't remotely want to explore, that just made her angry again.

"What?" he asked, clearly seeing the shift of her mood on her face.

"What about you and Feena, then? If I'm in so much danger, what about you?"

"You know I'm immune to their effects," Fitz said.

"I know you've said so," she said. "You've been spending a lot of time with her since last year. A lot of time. If you're reporting anything back to Colonel Hansen, I haven't heard a bit of it."

"Nothing to report," Fitz said with a shrug, then looked around before choosing a direction to continue walking in.

"You seem to enjoy your time with her," Ritchie said. She hoped the growing lump in her throat wasn't audible in her voice.

"I've been doing as I was asked," Fitz said. He shot her a quick sideways glance as if to gauge her current anger level, then said, "like I told you, a lot of things are waiting for me to talk to my father. It's not a happy place for me, waiting on things I can't control. Spending time with Feena feels like at least a productive thing I can do in the meantime."

"That's what all the kissing has been about? Feeling productive?" Ritchie regretted the words the minute they were out of her mouth.

Now it was Fitz pulling her to a stop to look her in the eye. But this time, she had no idea what was going on in his mind.

"I don't understand that question," he said at last. "I mean, what do you even care?"

"We're friends. I worry," Ritchie said, but he was already shaking his head at that.

"No, you just said we weren't."

"I was angry," Ritchie said.

"And now you're what?" he asked. The corner of his mouth twitched, but he didn't quite smile at her.

"Worried," she said, over-enunciating the word for him.

"Well, you have no reason to be worried," Fitz said, and immediately started walking away from her again. Ritchie jogged to catch up. The minute she fell into step beside him, he shot her another side-eye then said, "I mean, you're the one with a boyfriend. Right?"

"Right," Ritchie said, and felt a stab of guilt for the usual accumulation of messages from Guy that she had yet to respond to. But she summoned her anger again to say, "you could've remembered that before accusing me of falling under Finn's sway."

"I could've," Fitz agreed amicably. "Of course to Finn, that wouldn't have mattered at all."

"It matters to me," Ritchie pointed out.

"If Finn really wanted to, I think he could change that," Fitz said. There was a darkness in his tone now, like he was speaking his worst nightmare. "I know you don't agree, but I know he could. Maybe not permanently, but it wouldn't matter. If he nudged your mind just a little, there would be consequences."

"You have been very clear you don't want me to be alone with him again," Ritchie said.

"But you haven't agreed," he countered.

"And if I asked you to stay away from Feena? What then?" Ritchie shot back as they passed through another arched trellis to a little courtyard within the hedge maze.

"Then things would get a little awkward, wouldn't they?" a sad voice asked.

Ritchie and Fitz both pulled up short to stare at Feena, suddenly there with them. She was sitting on a wide stone bench in the center of the hedge-bordered space.

"Were you waiting for us?" Ritchie demanded.

"Yes, I was," Feena said. "I figured you'd come this way."

"How did you know that?" Ritchie asked.

"My location is public," Fitz reminded her, and Feena nodded.

"Whatever ramble you were taking, you'd have to come back this way to get to either your dormitory or to one of the schools," she said.

"What do you want?" Ritchie asked, still nearly shouting everything as if it were a command.

"Let me take this," Fitz said to her, then walked over to sit on the bench with Feena. There was a wide space between them, but it still felt all of a sudden like Ritchie was intruding on their moment instead of the other way around.

"I wanted to talk to you about Nils," Feena said to Fitz. Her hands fluttered like she wanted to reach out and take his, but he kept his hands clasping the elbows of his crossed arms, inaccessible.

"There was something between you," Ritchie said. She was completely unwilling to pretend to be invisible or worse, just leave them alone together.

"Not really," Feena said, and gave Ritchie a soft smile. "I know he had feelings for me, of course. It was pretty obvious. But I never encouraged him. And, of course, the rumor mill has me firmly in the 'taken' column. I was hoping that would be enough to keep him away. But he never seemed to find that any impediment."

"Was he obsessive?" Fitz asked her.

"With me? No, never," Feena said.

Ritchie scoffed out loud. Feena frowned at that, but Fitz cleared his throat to keep her attention on him.

"The first time I met him, he was glaring daggers at me," he told her. "What did that mean?"

"I honestly don't know," Feena said. "I just wanted you to know I never encouraged anything from him or anyone else. There is absolutely no reason anyone would kill anyone else over me. Not by any actions I've taken, I mean."

"You, of course, can't be held accountable for actions you just... inspire," Ritchie said.

"Of course not," Fitz said to Feena, but he shot Ritchie an incredulous look.

Oh, right. She was doing just the opposite of what she had said she'd do. She was descending to the lowest level all because she didn't trust the Berwegers.

"Do you know anyone else that might have a reason?" Fitz asked.

"I wish I did," Feena said glumly. "I want to help you. Both of you, of course. Ritchie, however you may feel, I consider you a friend."

"Just between friends, then, tell your brother to back off," Ritchie said.

Feena gave her a confused look, then turned to Fitz.

"She means... well, just what she said," Fitz told her.

"Oh. Of course. Well, I can certainly talk to him. Beyond that, I can't make any promises," Feena said. "I have to get back to class now. Just tell me you believe me?"

Fitz finally let her grasp both of his hands. "I believe you," he said.

She radiated happiness at him, then left the courtyard.

"Do you?" Ritchie asked, not sure she even wanted to hear the answer.

"Don't you?" he asked.

Ritchie thought it over. Then she sighed heavily. "Unfortunately, yes. From all I've heard of Nils Kaufmann, I doubt very much he had tipped over into obsession in the few weeks he's been in the presence of Feena Berweger. And if she had been putting the whammy on him, his behavior would've been so altered everyone would be remarking on it."

"So she wasn't involved," Fitz said.

"But I don't think Finn was either," Ritchie said.

"Well, that sucks," Fitz said, and kicked at a tuft of grass.

Ritchie had to agree. If the Berwegers weren't suspects, they had no suspects. They had no clues. They had no leads.

And with Wyss on the far side of the Union of Free Worlds, they had no way of finding out if the crime investigation unit had any of those things either.

All they could do was what they had come to Braga to do in the first place. Visit a couple of post-academy schools.

And that just felt pointless.

20

WHEN THEY REACHED THE DORMITORIES, Ritchie had mumbled something about a nap, then headed up the stairs towards the rooms. Fitz let her go. He could see she was exhausted by the lines on her face, even if her all-over-the-place emotions weren't tipping him off. She needed that nap.

But for his part, he wasn't remotely tired. He decided instead to head back to the diplomat school, to the scene of the crime.

The minute he tried to climb the steps up to the patio, he got his first taste of how his implant was programmed to warn him off. A flashing message about not crossing the boundaries of a crime scene obscured his vision, a loud whine that existed only in his own ears echoed through his skull, and there was a terrible taste in his mouth like he'd been sucking on leaky batteries.

He backed away, then tripped and fell. He stayed there for a moment, sprawled out on the cool if prickly grass of the lawn, and waited for the implant's warning mode to run its course.

Then he waited a little longer for the stabbing pain in his temples to ease.

Only then did he push himself to his feet and walk further along a gravel path to a second, lower doorway into the diplomat school.

It was late in the afternoon, and judging from the droning voices he could hear echoing down the hallways, some classes were still in session. But there were also cadets walking through the corridors, apparently done for the day. Not a one of them looked remotely relaxed, though. They all clutched their tablets tight to their chests and marched with purpose to wherever they were going. A couple were even mumbling to themselves.

Fitz found himself back in the tree-lined library. He again saw Leodegrance Kung sitting alone at a workstation. He was resting his head on one hand, ostensibly studying the tablet on the desk in front of him. But the minute Fitz came in the room, he sat up and waved.

"Hey," Fitz said in a low, library-appropriate voice as he dragged over a nearby chair. "I saw you during the tour, but not at the party after."

"No, I was busy," Kung said, gesturing at his schoolwork.

"Enjoying it here?" Fitz asked.

"It's great," Kung said, perhaps too brightly.

"I'm on the tours for both, but I've pretty much come down on the guardian side," Fitz told him. "Just curious about your honest assessment. This place looks brutal."

"It's challenging," Kung admitted. "But I don't mind that, really. The classes are so interesting, I don't even mind that the workload is so intense."

"Really?" Fitz asked skeptically.

"Really," Kung insisted. But then something passed over his face.

"What?" Fitz asked.

"Nothing," Kung said at once. But when Fitz just kept staring at him, he went on, "I mean, the culture here isn't great. It's not anything the instructors are doing, mind you. I think it's something that just generated itself spontaneously among the cadets. This many driven people all in one place, deciding that they're competing with each other. It isn't always good."

"Yeah, that's been brought to my attention," Fitz said. "Is everyone about to snap or what?"

"Some manage the stress better than others," Kung said. But he blew out an exasperated breath. "But there's no reason for it to be like this, is there? We're all looking to achieve the same thing: to be the best we can be and to work together to make the Union the best it can be. A little healthy competition is one thing, but we shouldn't be killing each other to achieve that goal."

"Killing each other?" Fitz repeated.

All the blood rushed out of Kung's face. "I'm so sorry. I forgot about what happened."

"I didn't think you were rubbing it in," Fitz said. "I just wondered if you thought this school was the reason why that happened."

"Oh. I hadn't thought about it," Kung said. Then the blood rushed back into his face, turning it a brilliant shade of red.

"You just thought murders happened wherever I went," Fitz guessed.

"Actually, I was going to say 'wherever Ritchie went'," Kung admitted sheepishly.

"I'm pretty sure we stumbled into the middle of something that doesn't exactly involve us," Fitz said.

"I suppose that's true most of the time," Kung said.

"I'd like to think so," Fitz said. "But back to what you said before. Is this really killing each other level, the competitive spirit here?"

"I don't know. I've only been here a few weeks," Kung said.

"Give me your impressions, then," Fitz said.

"There's a real dark side to diplomatic work," Kung said to him in a low voice. He glanced around, but none of the other cadets working in the library were within earshot. Even so, he pulled his chair closer to Fitz's. "They teach us how to mask our emotions. To be always outwardly calm and logical. Some species react very badly to the emotional responses of others, right?"

"Yeah, we learned a little of that at the academy," Fitz reminded him, deciding not to mention the class that morning. He wanted to know what Kung thought about it all.

"Oh, this is a whole other level," Kung said. "This isn't just holding your breath and counting to ten until the anger passes. This is actively repressing your own emotions. Seriously, you put it all away to unpack later when you're alone, preferably after the mission is done. We start that training day one."

"That does sound dark," Fitz agreed, "but I'm not sure if it's relevant."

"It's not part of the curriculum, at least not at my level, but some of the cadets have worked out how the techniques they teach us to self-regulate can be worked on others. To manipulate their emotions, but subtly."

Fitz considered this. "But if that were true, you all know it. You said the training starts on day one, right?"

"You'd be surprised," Kung said. "A driven cadet can work mind games on a weaker cadet. I've seen it happen. All the time." He sighed and rubbed at his forehead. "It's not what I was expecting when I started here. I really thought there'd be more of a team environment."

"There ought to be," Fitz said. "Like you said, we're all working towards the same goal. We'll be doing it in the future as full-fledged guardians and diplomats. It should be happening here too."

"Right? I don't understand why everything is so wrong here," he said miserably.

"I suppose the Berwegers are fitting right in, then?" Fitz asked.

"It's very much their sort of place," Kung agreed. "I mean, so far, no one really likes them much. But they don't really care about that. And it's not even important for what we do here. Respect matters so much more than affection, and their skills are such they always command respect."

"Yeah," Fitz said. "Do you have squads here like the guardians do?"

"We barely even have buddies," Kung said. "I have one who was assigned to me, and we bunk together and everything, but it's not the same as what it was like with me and Blaser."

"It's only been a few weeks," Fitz said.

"Even so. Not the same," Kung said.

"I saw Blaser while I was in lockup, actually," Fitz said. "He said he's been trying to message you. You know, at the guardian school, they have a meetup of former Oymyakon cadets. Nothing terribly formal, just the sort of get together where whoever is free just drops in. I know he'd love to see you."

"I should probably do that," Kung said, looking down at his schoolwork. "I've been avoiding it in favor of staying here and studying, but I'm not sure if that's where my energy should be going."

"Friends are important," Fitz said.

"Sure, but besides that, I can already tell my skill level isn't high enough to be top of the class," Kung said.

"So?" Fitz asked, genuinely flummoxed by that statement. "You do your best, right? That's literally what you just said a minute ago."

"I said that's what it *should* be like," Kung said, still scowling down at his tablets. "What it's actually like is that there's no reason for any of this if you're not going to be the top of the class."

"That's crazy," Fitz said. "There's no way this school is run with the idea that only one cadet matters in the end. Maybe you need to talk to a counselor or something about all this. If it's true, a lot of things need to be changed."

"I've been told it's the culture here and I have to adapt," Kung said.

"By who?" Fitz asked.

"Everyone," Kung said. Which, as far as Fitz could tell, just meant a bunch of people who weren't counselors or instructors or anyone with the power to make the changes that needed to be made.

Fitz fought back the sudden urge to become a diplomat. He couldn't make a lifelong career choice based on a sudden desire to turn one school's culture around.

But it was certainly tempting.

"It's be the best or be nothing," Kung said, fiddling with his stylus. "Second place just means first loser. Honestly, if it weren't too late, I'd switch to the guardian school right now."

Fitz had still been musing over his desire to turn things around, pondering whether he, as a visitor, could get a minute of anyone's time who could change things, when something Kung said caught his attention. "What did you just say?"

"That I'd switch to guardian school if I could?" Kung said, and was about to continue moaning on that topic, but Fitz just shook his head.

"No, before that," he said.

"I don't know," Kung shrugged.

"You said second place is just first loser," Fitz said.

"Here, that's true," Kung said. "So?"

"So I think you just handed me a motive," Fitz said, already pushing up from the table to run he knew not where.

It was an important breakthrough, sure. The murder victim was the top of the class, the only one who mattered in the eyes of his fellow diplomat cadets. This made suspects out of everyone else in his class, if not the whole school.

But maybe not. Maybe the cadet who felt this distinction the most keenly was the one who didn't see themselves as second place.

Who here was the first loser?

Fitz didn't know where to start, except he had to go wake up Ritchie.

They had a lot of cadets to question.

21

THE SUN WAS SETTING FAR TOO QUICKLY, and it was taking all the warmth with it. It was like someone had thrown a switch, and warm breezes that had felt so nice stirring Ritchie's hair off her sweaty brow were gone in an instant, replaced by a cold wind that chilled her still-damp brow.

"I don't know if I could ever get used to this," Ritchie said, hugging her arms close and wishing she had brought a jacket with her. Now she knew why the diplomat cadets all carried oversized bags with them everywhere. It was only partly to haul around the variety of incompatible tablets their studies required them to use. The few other people she could see in the gardens with her and Moreau were all pulling out sweaters and scarves and carrying on as if the sudden chill were perfectly normal.

Which, for Braga, it probably was.

"Here," Moreau said, and placed something warm and soft onto the palm of her hand.

It was a piece of fruit. The same kind of fruit she had eaten on the walk from the station to the dormitory. Ritchie gave her a thankful smile, then bit deeply into the sweet, juicy flesh.

"I don't know where we're even supposed to be for dinner," she admitted as she caught a dribble of juice with the side of her hand before it could drip off her chin and onto her uniform.

"In the dormitories. Just a casual thing today," Moreau told her. "You weren't at your sociology class, were you?"

"No, I was at the guardian school. Then Fitz and I were just walking around and we ran into Feena," she said.

"You can run into anyone in these hedges," Moreau said. "No warning ahead of time, just all of a sudden you're face to face with anyone at all."

"You've noticed that too?" Ritchie said, as she tossed the core under a bush. Then she heard a sound like a sucking in of breath. She motioned for Moreau to not make a sound as she stood there, trying to discern where it was coming from.

It took a moment, but then Moreau heard it too. They listened, and Ritchie knew it was someone crying, but she couldn't tell from where.

Then Moreau pointed down a narrow break in the hedges a little further up the path. Ritchie headed that way, poking her head inside a space she wasn't sure was meant to be an opening.

It was another one of the little courtyards with a bench between two potted plants. But it definitely wasn't Feena this time. No, that long spill of loose black hair could only belong to one person.

"Hefti?" Ritchie called as she stepped through the hedge and into the courtyard. Hefti lifted her face at once, then scrubbed vigorously at her cheeks.

At least she didn't instantly insist that she hadn't been crying. Although she seemed determined to act as if she hadn't.

"Are you cadets lost?" she asked, looking from Ritchie to Moreau, then back again.

"No, just taking a slow walk back to the dormitories," Ritchie said. "Are you all right?"

"Perfectly," she said, but she wiped at her cheeks again, delicately with the back of her hand, as if to be sure they were dry.

"You know, you made a strong impression on my friend this morning," Ritchie said.

"Your friend?" Hefti said with a little frown.

"Cadet Fitz," Ritchie said. "In the emotion control class."

"Oh, him. Yes, I suppose I saw you come over after, so you two must be friends," she said, but she sounded distant. Like she was really talking to herself and not to Ritchie. But then she focused on her and Moreau again, and her frown deepened. "He said he was going to be a guardian?"

"Yes, but he still liked the class," Ritchie said. "He said everyone should take a class like that, no matter what school they go to."

Hefti was still frowning as if she were attempting to do complex math in her head.

"We interrupted something," Moreau said, putting a hand on Ritchie's hand to draw her away.

"No, I was just thinking," Hefti said.

"I'm sorry we keep intruding on you when you're clearly having a private moment," Ritchie said. She bit her tongue before she could say the rest of what she was thinking, about the need to find private places for a private moment.

The courtyard they were standing in was pretty far from everything and ought to have been a more secluded place than even Hefti's room at the school, where she almost certainly had a roommate, if not three.

"No worries," Hefti said, but she still looked like the wheels of her mind were spinning furiously. "Your friend Fitz had a lot of questions."

"He's like that," Ritchie agreed.

"About Nils Kaufmann," Hefti said. "Why would he think I knew anything about Nils Kaufmann?"

"It seems like everyone knew Nils Kaufmann," Ritchie said. "I gather he was very popular."

"Yes, not like me," Hefti said, but with no malice. Just an observation.

"He was sitting next to Kaufmann when he died, you know," Moreau said. "He tried to save him."

"Yes," Hefti said. "Such a shame. That's probably why he was asking, right? Just curious?"

Ritchie chewed at her lip. Had she found the one person who didn't know that she and Fitz investigated murders? No, that couldn't be true. Unlike with Moreau, Hefti always remembered Ritchie's name. There was usually only one reason for that.

But Hefti was giving them a chagrined smile now. "I'm sorry you keep catching me at a bad moment. I've had a bad few days. But honestly, it's not really a school issue, I promise you."

"Sure," Ritchie said guardedly. It felt like a delicate thing, talking with Hefti. Like handling a bomb without the proper equipment. It could explode at any moment.

"It's a shame about the dinner party, actually," she said. Then blushed as if she had misspoken. "I don't mean… well, obviously Nils dying is beyond a shame."

"Sure," Ritchie said again.

"But I meant, the evening was supposed to end with a tea ceremony. Very elaborate. There are sixteen different utensils used to prepare the tea, and every gesture has to be just so." Then she blushed again, only this time she covered her cheeks with her hands as if she could hide that reaction. "I know it's not really anything of importance in the grander scheme of things, but the protocol for that ceremony was my end-of-year project last year. I worked so hard on it. It was amazing when it was chosen for this big event. And no one ever saw it."

"I can see why you're disappointed," Ritchie said.

"She's just saying that because she loves tea," Moreau said.

"Do you?" Hefti asked eagerly. Her eyes darted in that way that said she was checking the chronometer on her implant. "Dinner is still about an hour away. Would you like to come back to my room and sample some? I don't have time for the full ceremony, but I can give you a sense of what it would've looked like. And you'll definitely enjoy the tea."

"It's not smoky, is it?" Ritchie asked.

"No, it's floral-based," Hefti said. "Very delicate, almost like a jasmine? I think you'll like it. But I can throw some sugar in if you like."

"No, not without tasting it first," Ritchie said.

"Great! Oh, thanks so much, you guys," Hefti said as she got up from the bench, then led them back through the hedge maze to the diplomat school. "I know it seems like nothing, but it means a lot to me."

"Should I mention I'm not a fan of tea?" Moreau whispered to Ritchie.

"Get used to it," Ritchie hissed back. "If you want to be a diplomat, you're going to have to drink all sorts of things."

"That's true," Moreau said.

They climbed the steps, the marble gleaming in the light of dozens of floating orbs that hung just overhead to light the way. Then they were in the main hall, where the lights were hidden in the leaves of the trees around them, much like in the hedge maze.

Hefti started down a corridor then drew up short so suddenly that both Ritchie and Moreau nearly collided with her. She lifted a finger to her lips to signal for silence, and they all three melted back into the shadows just before Feena Berweger passed by.

She was on her own and looked like she was distracted by something, but she never noticed them there. She headed out the main door, out into the gardens. Then Hefti signaled for them to continue down the hall.

"Sorry, I just don't like her," she said.

"Believe me, we get that," Moreau assured her.

They climbed two flights of stairs and emerged in a corridor that was on one side lined with doors and on the other was open to overlook a courtyard below. They continued to the point where the corridor took a 90-degree turn to continue around the courtyard, but Hefti stopped at the last door there and touched her hand to the doorknob to unlock it before turning it to let them in.

"My roommate is in the library cramming before dinner, so she won't interrupt us," Hefti said as she waved her hand to turn on a few lights that beamed up towards the tiled ceiling, only spilling an indirect light on the tidy room below.

"I missed the dormitory part of the tour," Moreau said as she looked around the room. "Why didn't they lead with that? If all the rooms are like this, this is definitely the school for me."

"Oh?" Hefti said, looking around as if noticing the room for the first time. Two beds were tucked away in smaller rooms that were separated from the main space by doors of wood that looked like they had been woven like baskets. It was a beautiful effect.

The room itself was all rugs and pillows, with a few low desks designed to be used by someone sitting on the floor. Beyond that was the ubiquitous patio overlooking the gardens.

"These are a little nicer than most because we're last-years, but really only a little nicer. I'll have to see if I can find a first-year who will show you their room. You should definitely see that. In the meantime, please sit! Any pillow will do."

Ritchie and Moreau sat down on flat but surprisingly comfortable pillows. Hefti set one of the desks between them, then turned to open a pair of cabinet doors in the wall opposite the patio to reveal an entire kitchenette.

"So, are you both thinking you'll come here next year?" she asked as she first got water boiling inside a pot on the narrow counter, then began assembling the sixteen utensils on her tea tray.

"I'm not sure," Ritchie admitted. Moreau just shrugged, which of course Hefti with her back to them couldn't see. But as usual, Hefti seemed to forget there were two of them there with her. She was a strange sort of girl.

"Oh, I do hope you decide to come here," Hefti said, setting the tray on top of the desk between them. Ritchie looked over the arrangement of items on the tray and admitted to herself she really didn't know what most of them did. The teapot was self-explanatory, but what were the tongs for?

Hefti went back for the water. Moreau picked up a little whisk and examined it, then hastily put it back down before Hefti returned with the boiling water. But she just set the kettle on the ground as she knelt down facing the two of them.

"The ceremony has a lot of steps, but do you mind if I just condense them a little? Most of them are just theatrics and don't really affect the taste of the tea. Unless you like theatrics?" she asked eagerly.

But Ritchie had a sudden feeling that she wanted to talk to Fitz about something. Or maybe vice versa. But he was at the dormitory by now, getting ready for dinner.

"Just the tea, I think," she said, and Hefti failed to hide her disappointment.

"Of course," she said and summoned up a smile as she mixed four different powdery teas together inside the pot and then poured the water over them until it deliberately overflowed the sides of the clay pot. Then she put the lid over it. "It just takes a moment."

"So you don't like Feena?" Ritchie said to fill the time. Moreau had picked up a spoon and was turning it over in her hands, examining some detail carved into the handle in the dim light.

"Does anyone?" Hefti said, then flushed. "That's unkind."

"But true," Moreau said, setting the spoon down but picking up one of the saucers. "This feels weird. Not like porcelain or clay or anything. Ritchie, touch one."

Ritchie started to reach for a saucer, then looked up at Hefti to be sure they weren't ruining her moment even worse than before. But Hefti just gave her an encouraging nod, and Ritchie gently picked up the other saucer.

It did feel strange. Cold and porous, almost like it hadn't finished being formed.

"It's traditional among the species the guardians were pretending to be at the dinner party," Hefti said, then signaled for them to set them back on the tray so she could fill their cups.

"Your research was on their ceremony specifically?" Ritchie asked. Hefti nodded, her focus on filling the cups to the absolute brim without spilling a drop.

"Yes. I spent a semester on it. But it was all pointless in the end," Hefti said.

"Don't say that," Ritchie said, as Moreau took her first tentative sip from the cup that was too full to be lifted. She had to bend over and put her lips to the cup resting there on her saucer.

"No, it was pointless. It really was," Hefti said with a sigh. But then she motioned towards Moreau. "She actually knows how this is done, believe it or not."

"And it's really good," Moreau said as she paused in her sipping to look up at Ritchie.

Ritchie grabbed the handle of her cup to pivot it on the saucer into a better position, then bent forward and sipped gently.

Hefti was right. It was very like a sweet jasmine tea, or at least the flavor was. But it hit her brain in a rush that was completely unlike any tea she'd ever had. It was more like an uber coffee bomb, hitting her with sugar and caffeine at maximum levels all at once.

But this wasn't that. That was almost too much teeth-grinding energy all at once. This was softer, sweeter. Just a gentle lighting up of her brain.

"Well?" Hefti said, her hands at her mouth as she waited for Ritchie's response.

"S'good," Ritchie assured her.

But something was wrong. The light in the room had gotten brighter for a flash, but now it was darker. And it was dark in blots. Which didn't make sense.

"S'what kind tea?" she asked, or tried to. Her tongue was too thick to enunciate sounds.

She turned her head to look over at Moreau. That little motion almost sent her sprawling, like she didn't know her own strength.

That made the lights in the room flash again before the dark blobs returned.

So it took far too long for Ritchie to make out Moreau already sprawled out on the rug beside her.

Poison.

Ritchie started to giggle at the absurdity of it all. She had done it! She had found the poison by finding the poisoner!

But Moreau wasn't moving. She didn't even look like she was breathing. And the darkness was reaching out towards Ritchie now.

She tried to turn her head again to look at Hefti. Why wasn't she saying anything? She had brought the two of them back to her room specifically so she could poison them. Why wasn't she gloating?

But Ritchie couldn't quite lift her head or focus on Hefti's shifting form in her darkening vision.

She had made a mistake coming here. A bad mistake.

She remembered her implant and tried to send out a distress call. But keeping her implant always on the minimum use settings meant that took an extra step now.

One more step than she could do. She never even felt her face hit that pillow.

22

FITZ KNEW that Ritchie avoided using her implant when she could help it. But she never turned it off completely. It would be impossible for her to do that and remain a cadet.

So why couldn't his pings find her?

He would tell himself he was being paranoid if this exact thing didn't keep happening with her. And it was always bad news.

"What is it?" Kung asked. Fitz had forgotten Kung was there while he stood frozen in place, trying to contact Ritchie.

"I can't reach Ritchie," he said.

Kung was quiet for a moment, then said gravely, "I can't either. What does that mean?"

"Nothing good," Fitz said. Then a thought struck him. "Try Moreau."

"No response," Kung said after another long moment.

"Me neither," Fitz said. "I don't like this."

"Let me check with the school system," Kung said. "It tracks everyone's movements inside the building."

"Invasive much?" Fitz muttered. Then tried to reach the same system. His implant found it easily enough.

And immediately triggered a red flag. He wasn't allowed access, and the crime investigation unit had been informed that he had tried to use it.

Which maybe wasn't a bad thing. He sent a message directly to Colonel Hansen asking where Ritchie and Moreau were, but before he got a response, Kung said, "they went up to the dorms."

"Right, dinner," Fitz said, feeling stupid that he had missed the obvious.

"No, not your dormitory building. The dorms here," Kung said. He shoved his tablet into his bag and slung it over his shoulder. "I'll show you. I can follow them as far as the corridor they were in last, but I don't know which door they went through."

"Do you know which cadets they belong to?" Fitz asked, as he and Kung walked swiftly out of the library. The halls were empty, but he could hear voices distantly. Not so much the weird whispery thing, but more like laughter and chatting like at a party at the far end of the building. Dinner must be even more social here than lunch.

"They were on the floor where the last-year cadets have their rooms. A few were in the hall at about the same time, but I don't know exactly who they might have been with. The system doesn't track that way. I can get those names or the names of who dorms in those rooms, but I don't know which name would be significant. Would you?" Kung asked.

"Probably not," Fitz said.

"I can send you the list," Kung offered.

"Somehow, I think that would just set off my implant again," Fitz grumbled.

"Huh?"

"Never mind," Fitz said. Then he remembered his breakthrough, the reason he had been trying to contact Ritchie in the first place. "Kaufmann was top of the class, but now that he's dead, the second place cadet is top. Do you know who that is?"

"Of course. It's Hefti," Kung said as they ran up a narrow flight of stairs at a jog. "Her room is right where they disappeared."

"Then that's where we start," Fitz said.

He was still running when the stairs ended and the corridor began, but what had happened when he had tried to step onto the patio crime scene happened again, driving him to his knees as his implant very painfully informed him that the dorms were off limits.

"What's going on?" Kung asked in alarm as he tried to help Fitz back to his feet.

"I'm not supposed to be here," Fitz said through gritted teeth. He was pretty sure he was shouting, too. The noise in his ears was unbelievably intense. "But this is good. They'll come to take me back into custody. I just hope their response time is fast enough."

"It's at the end of the hall. Do you want me to go alone?" Kung asked. Fitz had managed a few stumbling steps, but as if being half-blinded wasn't bad enough, he was starting to feel a vicious sort of vertigo. The odds of him tumbling over the railing and down into the courtyard below were feeling a touch too high.

"Yeah," Fitz said, giving Kung a little push. "Get to her."

Kung gave him a nod, dropping his bag before sprinting to the end of the hall. Fitz slumped to the floor next to the bag and clutched at his head. His fingers dug deeply into his pounding temples, but he managed to hold it up to watch as Kung pounded at the door with his fist. He only waited for a moment for an answer, and when it didn't come, he started kicking at the door.

Then, all at once, all the noise and lights and vertigo in his head just went away. It was like he was suddenly thrust back into the real world, the only pounding sound Kung's boot on the stubborn door.

Then his implant lit up again, but only at a level he was used to. He had more than a dozen messages from Hansen and another dozen from Kasteler. He only gave those messages a scan, enough to know the two officers were both on their way, but the two of them shared his sense of alarm enough to where they had removed the lockdown on his implant.

He was free to move now.

He needed to move.

He struggled to get to his feet, then nearly fell again when someone running past him impacted with his shoulder. Then other hands were catching him, helping him to his feet and holding him until he was steady.

"Feena?" Fitz said when he realized it was she who was holding him up.

And it had been Finn who had bowled him over. Fitz started to run after him, but Finn was already at the door, pushing Kung aside so he could strike the door with a kick of his own.

The door splintered at once, breaking away from both the locking mechanism and from the hinges. It fell to the floor inside the dorm room with a thump, then Finn disappeared inside.

"Why are you here?" Fitz asked Feena as they ran towards the door.

"We've been monitoring your location," she said. "There's only one reason you'd come up this way. We're here to help."

"Great," Fitz said, but somehow that word didn't come out as sarcastically as he had meant it to.

Then they were inside the room. Kung was on one knee beside the prostrate form of Moreau, who laid motionless among the pillows. Finn was trying to sit Ritchie up, but her head was lolling back against his arm like she was broken doll.

"She did this!" Hefti said, pointing at Feena the moment she came in through the door. "She saw us all coming up here together, and she poisoned my tea."

"She saw you coming up to your dorm and got here first?" Fitz asked. "She broke into your room and poisoned the tea and disappeared again all before you three got here?"

"She barely has a pulse," Kung said as he touched the side of Moreau's neck.

"The authorities are already on the way," Fitz told him. "How's Ritchie?"

But Finn didn't answer. He was still clutching Ritchie close to his chest, but he just glared at Hefti with pure hate in his eyes. "You do this, and then you accuse my sister?"

"Why would I poison these two? They're your enemies. Yours and hers," Hefti said. But she backed away from his eyes, stopping only when she backed up against the wall and could go no further.

"You dare do this? And for what? A class rank?" Finn said, laying Ritchie back down so he could get to his feet. He wasn't shouting, he wasn't even exactly raising his voice, but that voice was filling the room in a way that rumbled painfully against Fitz's eardrums. He could see Kung flinching as well.

But Feena was unbothered by her brother's voice. She too advanced on Hefti, her hands in fists and her blue eyes filled with hate.

Fitz dropped down beside Kung and felt for Ritchie's pulse. He wasn't sure if he had it, or if he was imagining it. Maybe it was his own pulse because he was grasping her so tightly. But her flesh was cold, and her face was turning blue. He knew he wasn't imagining that.

"Veronika, look at me," Finn said, planting a hand on the wall over her shoulder and leaning in. She had no escape. She tried avoiding his eyes, then she tried looking to Feena for help. But Feena was just as angry as her brother, and once she locked eyes with Hefti, she didn't let her look away.

"You accuse me?" Feena said, and the air vibrated with her words.

"I don't know who did this, but it wasn't me," Hefti said, her voice squeaking in her fright.

"Why would I poison my dear friends?" Feena asked.

"I don't know. I just thought… I didn't know they were friends. I thought… the opposite, I guess," Hefti said.

"Friends is too small a word for what they are to us," Finn said. "Why would you do this? Tell me true, Veronika. Tell me why you hurt them."

"I… they… I…" But she had nothing.

"Ritchie figured out it was Hefti who killed Kaufmann," Fitz guessed. He forced his fingers to loosen their grip, then tried again to feel her pulse. This time, he was sure he wasn't imagining it. But it was a weak thing. How long would it take for help to arrive?

"Is this true, Veronika?" Feena asked, reaching out to touch Hefti's cheek almost fondly. Finn was still leaning in over her, his breath stirring the tendrils of hair that had come loose over her ear.

"No, she didn't," Hefti said defiantly. "She had no idea when she came up here. You were closer to figuring it out than she was. She didn't know a thing until she felt the poison start its work, and then it was far too late." She jutted her chin up and tried to turn the look she couldn't tear away from Feena's eyes into a glare.

"You knew we would be suspects when you took out Kaufmann, didn't you?" Finn asked. "That was your plan?"

"You were convenient. So was Fitz. Every other table at the banquet had four people around it. Every one but theirs. And no one at their table was even a guardian cadet playing the role of the visiting species. No one even noticed. Not even Kaufmann. Not even Fitz," Hefti said. Finn was touching her hair now, and almost as if she couldn't help herself, she shifted her gaze from Feena to Finn.

Fitz was pretty sure he didn't want to watch whatever was going to happen next. He had seen what the twins could do before, but he had never seen them do it when they were so angry.

He supposed he should feel angry too. Kaufmann might have been her target for murder, but she had definitely used him to obscure her hand in things. Because murders tended to happen wherever he and Ritchie went.

He had a right to feel angry. But all he felt was disgust. Disgust for Hefti, but fear for Ritchie motionless in his arms.

But then he heard boots in the corridor. "Come on," he said to Kung, then started dragging Ritchie out into the hallway to meet the authorities. He wanted to be sure she and Moreau were taken care of even before anyone tried to stop whatever the Berwegers were doing to Hefti up against that wall.

But that didn't make the knot of anxiety in his stomach any looser. He was pretty sure he was living a moment he would regret later. He knew he shouldn't be turning his back on any of this.

Hansen and Kasteler were the first at the door, quickly helping Fitz and Kung get Ritchie and Moreau out to where the medics could start working on them. Fitz wanted to stay by Ritchie's side, but Hansen held him back.

"Let them work, son," he said close to Fitz's ear.

"You have to stop them," Kung said, pointing back into the dorm room. "I have no idea what they're doing, but you have to stop it."

Kasteler frowned even as she drew her weapon and charged into the room. Fitz went in after her, Hansen close on his heels.

Hefti was sitting on the floor now, slumped against the wall with a glazed look to her eyes. Finn and Feena were both kneeling beside her, each holding one of her hands. It looked like they were caring for her, making sure she was okay. But he knew that wasn't the case.

They were the reason that blood was trickling out of both of Hefti's ears. They were the reason her dark blue eyes were marred with hemorrhages, and the pupils were no longer the same size.

"Is she dead?" Kasteler asked as she put her weapon away. Apparently, the image of the twins caring for Hefti had convinced her that was what was happening.

"They did this," Fitz hissed at Hansen. Hansen just nodded, but held up a hand for Fitz to stay silent.

Hefti sat motionless for a long moment. Then she tipped and rolled her head until one of her mismatched pupils managed to focus on Kasteler. "I would like to go to prison now, chief inspector," she said in a gurgling voice. Then she coughed and spit blood up into her lap. "Please."

"She'll be all right," Finn said as he stepped back from Hefti. He was back to looking like a beatific angel and speaking with the warm tones to match. Fitz could see the crime investigation officers around him physically relax at his words.

"What happened to her?" Kasteler asked even as another two medics came in the door with med kits.

"Be careful what you touch," Feena said. Unlike her brother, she was still speaking in angry, commanding tones, and every officer froze in place at her words. "Veronika Hefti is a first-rate poisoner. Top of the class. But Fitz didn't spill antidote over everything this time. I assure you every implement on that tray and perhaps other things in this room are laced with a plethora of deadly agents. Nothing has been neutralized yet."

"It was on the service ware, not the food or drink," Finn told them. "And she didn't spike anything with the antidote this time, but I'm sure it's somewhere in this room."

"You have evidence enough to put her away now," Feena said.

"She looks like this because she poisoned herself?" Kasteler guessed.

Finn just smiled benignly at her. Feena turned away from the whole scene and swept out of the room. No one moved to stop her.

"Ritchie?" Fitz said to Hansen.

"She's at the medical facility getting care, as is Moreau," Hansen told him. "They got there in plenty of time. Their condition is already stable. Come, we're not needed here. Let's step aside and let the authorities take it from here."

"Yes, sir," Fitz said.

Finn locked eyes with Fitz, but Fitz couldn't discern any meaning in that gaze.

Except that Finn was still angry. So very angry. Was that really just because his sister was being accused of something she hadn't done? Or was there something more going on?

Fitz didn't like that thought at all. It felt too much like Ritchie was an important piece in Finn Berweger's machinations, and that didn't bode well.

That didn't bode well at all.

$$23$$

RITCHIE KNEW she had woken a few times before. She had vague memories of opening her eyes and even moving her body around, holding out an arm or whatever for one of the medical techs to do something or other. But they were short memories, almost like fragments of dreams if her dreams were ever so mundane.

But this time was different. This time, when she dragged her eyelids open over her itchy, dry eyes, she felt more alert than those times before. She could feel the warmth of the sun on the right side of her body and the breeze playing with her hair. She could see a table next to her bed, dominated by a single massive arrangement of flowers in rich jewelly colors she didn't even know existed. And just beyond the flowers, another bed containing a still sleeping Moreau.

She looked smaller than usual. Maybe because her hair was out of its topknot and lay loose over her pillow. Maybe because that pillow was so massive, it was like she disappeared into it. But Ritchie could see some of that blonde hair stirring as Moreau breathed.

Her own mouth still had a taste to it like the last remnants of that tea still lingered on her tongue but were overwhelmed by the bitter taste from the poison.

She hadn't tasted the poison at the time, but she certainly did now.

The breeze picked up, twisting strands of her hair into her eyelashes. She blinked them away, but something else caught her attention.

The breeze didn't smell like flowers. It smelled like woodchips and spice. The aroma was so familiar it brought a rush of memories that flooded her mind. Memories from her childhood back on Buennagel. Memories from that time before everything had gone so wrong.

"Fitz?" she said as she turned over to look towards the window.

But the person on the chair next to her bed wasn't Fitz. It was Finn.

His sister was there as well, fussing over another arrangement of flowers that stood on a table between the two open doorways that led out to another garden.

"How are you feeling?" Finn asked, reaching for her hand. But Ritchie snatched it back before he could touch her. "Sorry. I know I'm not who you wanted to see. But I believe he's on his way."

"Soon," Feena said from behind him, her attention still focused on the flowers.

"Fitz?" Ritchie said again, just to be sure they were all on the same page.

"Oh, I thought we were talking about Guy," Feena said, turning away from the flowers to face Ritchie. "Fitz is in detention again. He violated the terms of his parole."

"We've offered him the use of our family lawyers, but he insists that the colonel has it under control," Finn said. Then he laughed, "I think his release might get processed faster if he hadn't picked as his advocate the one person who would find any excuse to linger in the company of the chief inspector."

"He's safe," Feena said with a stern look for her brother. "That's all that matters."

"Yes, he's safe," Finn agreed. Then he smiled at Ritchie with warm fondness. "And so are you."

"What's going on here?" Ritchie asked. She tried to sit up, but her trembling limbs betrayed her. In the end, she had to allow Finn to hold her up as Feena fluffed up the pillows behind her until they supported her. But she couldn't bring herself to thank them for it.

There was something about their voices, something that was trying to trigger a memory, but she couldn't quite summon it forth. It was like she had heard those voices in some nightmare she had had while she was out. She couldn't bring up the memory, but the terror was right there, waiting to engulf her.

"What happened?" Ritchie asked. She was talking to herself, but it was Finn who answered her.

"You cleared our names," Finn said. "We wanted to be sure to thank you for that before you went back to Oymyakon."

"We've been here every day waiting for you to wake up so we could say thank you," Feena said.

"How long?" Ritchie asked.

"Four days," Feena told her, wincing in sympathy even before Ritchie could work out what that meant.

"The rest of your class has gone home already," Finn told her. "But the colonel stayed to wait for you two to recover and for Fitz to be released."

"I'm sure that will be any day now," Feena said, catching Ritchie's hand and giving it a squeeze before she could pull it away. "Maybe even today. They really have nothing to hold him on now."

If Ritchie had to guess, Hansen had convinced Kasteler to hold Fitz for any charge at all, because he knew Fitz would never go back without her.

But that thought was quickly trumped by another one.

"It *was* Hefti," Ritchie said, pressing a trembling hand to her forehead. She remembered going up to Hefti's room for tea, and she remembered realizing that Hefti was the murderer. But she didn't remember all the details in between. "Did I not figure that out until it was too late?" she moaned.

"Almost," Feena said cheerily.

"You gave us all a scare," Finn said.

"Did I?" Ritchie said skeptically.

"Finn kicked down the door to rescue you," Feena said.

"Now, sister, in all fairness, Kung was there first," he said.

"Kung and Fitz," Feena corrected him. "It wasn't Fitz's fault that his paroled implant incapacitated him."

"But it was Fitz that Hefti was afraid was about to figure it all out.

She really thought he had all the pieces," Finn said. "That she had been the top of the class the year before, until Kaufmann's final project on military history beat out her own work on… table arranging, was it?"

"Something like that," Feena said. "And anyway, I think Ritchie was closer. She was right there, wasn't she? Even Hefti must have thought so, when she went out into the maze to lure Ritchie and Moreau into her trap with her tears. She didn't do that to Fitz, did she?"

"I'm getting this story all in jumbled pieces here, aren't I?" Ritchie said.

"Sorry," Feena said with a smile. "We agreed to let Fitz tell it to you. That felt appropriate considering the bond you two have with each other. But he's still not out yet."

"We just wanted to be sure to thank you before you got whisked away," Finn said.

"Does the colonel know you're here in this room?" Ritchie asked.

She knew the answer even before they both grinned at her and Feena said, "of course not."

"We aren't here to hurt you, Ritchie," Finn said. "Honestly, when will you realize that?"

"You didn't kill Kaufmann. I'll agree on that score," Ritchie said.

"That's a start," Feena said to her brother.

"I suppose," he said, but he didn't sound cheered.

"We also wanted to talk to you about coming to the school with us next year," Feena said.

"I was going to say that," Finn said to her. She just shrugged, never taking her eyes off Ritchie. Finn grabbed Ritchie's hand, this time catching it before she could pull it away.

Then he leaned in, sitting on the edge of her bed and blocking her view of everything that wasn't him. "I know this is almost an impossible ask of you, but forget everything that's happened over the last years. Think back to the girl you were when you still had a father there at your dinner table every night. Picture that girl in your head."

Then he passed his free hand down over her eyes until she closed them. But she resisted his command to imagine anything. She just sat, waiting for him to finish.

"Picture that girl, and now advance her through the years. That girl gets accepted to the foreign service academy which is her first choice, and she does it on the first try. Because she's qualified and she's earned it. Picture her four years there at that academy. No one dies, no murders need to be investigated in order to clear her name or anyone else's. Do you see her?"

Ritchie said nothing. The breeze picked up again, and she could hear wind chimes somewhere in the gardens outside the doors.

She still smelled that Fitz smell of woodchips and spice, but she did her best to ignore that.

"Now that you have her firmly fixed in her mind, go ahead and open your eyes."

She really wanted to disobey that order. But that impulse felt childish, and not in keeping with her ultimate goal of getting rid of the Berwegers as quickly as she could.

She opened her eyes and was caught by Finn's eyes, the exact color of the sky over the prairies on Buennagel.

"Now tell me you don't have a deep calling to be a diplomat," he said. He was smiling triumphantly, as if she had already answered.

"I'm still not sure," Ritchie said, and that smile faltered.

"I am," Moreau said from the next bed over. Feena went over to her to help get her propped up on pillows. Then Moreau brushed the long strands of blond hair out of her face and looked around at all of them, her eyes bright and alert. "I'm in. Diplomat all the way."

"Really?" Ritchie asked.

"Really," Moreau said firmly.

"Well, I'm still not sure," Ritchie said to her.

"You don't have a lot of time to figure it out," Moreau reminded her.

But before she could answer, Feena said, "we don't have time ourselves."

Finn's eyes shifted to one side as he consulted something on his implant. Then he sighed before smiling into Ritchie's eyes again. "We *do* have to go. Undeclared will have to be my answer for now, won't it?"

"Tick-tock, Finn," Feena said even as she headed towards the doors that opened out onto the garden.

"Be right with you," Finn tossed over his shoulder. Then he said to Ritchie, "I have just one last thing to do here."

Before Ritchie could ask him what that was, his hands were in her hair as he kissed her. Thoroughly and deeply. Despite the fact that she tasted a little like jasmine tea and a lot like sour poison and bitter bile.

He broke away slowly and murmured something in her ear about hoping that would help her make up her mind. She didn't really hear it. Her ears were humming strangely.

Then she came back to herself with a jerk, the spell broken the moment she realized it was a spell. She sat up straighter in the bed as the anger rushed through her. But she knew there was no way she was going to be able to spring out of it and confront him. He didn't even look back at her as he followed his sister out into the garden.

But he did pause there for a moment, to whisper something in Fitz's ear.

Wait, Fitz was there? Was that what that kiss had been about? Getting under Fitz's skin?

But Fitz wasn't even looking at her. He was looking across the room to the other doorway, the one that lead further into the medical building. And all the color had drained from his face.

Ritchie pivoted to look the other way, but there was nothing there but an empty doorway. A single medical technician bustled by as she stared, but they didn't linger or even notice her.

"Oh, Ritchie," Moreau said, her voice wrenched with sadness.

"What?" Ritchie asked. She was blinking back tears, and she didn't even know why. What had just happened?

"Guy," Moreau said to her unasked question. "Guy saw. Then he left."

"Guy? But—"

But nothing made sense. Ritchie turned back towards the gardens, but the Berwegers were gone. And so was Fitz.

Ritchie swallowed down the bitter taste in her mouth, then activated her implant to send a hasty message to Guy.

Come back. That was just Finn being Finn. That wasn't about me at all. Please, come back. I can't get out of this bed. Guy?

Ritchie chewed at her lip aggressively as she waited for a response.

I can't do this now. he finally sent back.

Please come back. I've waited all week to see you, and you came all this way.

Again, it took forever to get a response back, and when she finally got it, she wished she hadn't.

I can't do this, Murdina. You're caught up in things that frankly scare me. I'm not coming back. My family may be rich, but we're not that powerful. I can't do this. Please understand.

Then, a moment later, was the worst of all.

Good-bye.

24

THE SECOND FOUR days Fitz spent in detention were far less tolerable than the first few had been. He had seen Hansen every day, and Hansen had promised to update him the instant he knew anything more about Ritchie and Moreau's condition besides "stable."

But it had been a lot of hours with nothing to do but stare at the ceiling and wait and wonder if Ritchie would ever wake up again.

And wonder why Finn had been so angry.

Occasionally, he would spare a thought or two to wonder about his own future now that he had a violation of parole charge to add to his destruction of a crime scene charge.

But then he'd go right back to one of the first two merry-go-rounds.

He wasn't sure why it didn't seem to matter to anyone that he had deliberated violated the blocks on his implant specifically to get help to come in a hurry. Chief Inspector Kasteler assured him that she believed him. But he was pretty sure that didn't mean she cared.

When they finally came to let him out, he barely bothered to listen to the explanations of what had changed. Something about a judge and strings that Colonel Hansen had tweaked if not outright pulled. All charges were dropped, and his record was clean.

He didn't care. The minute he was free, he ran at a full sprint all the way to the medical building.

He was halfway there when Hansen pinged him with a quick message that Ritchie was awake and Moreau was about to come to as well. Fitz leaned in and forced his legs to keep running. Frankly, after days pacing the length of a single room, it felt good to run for all he was worth.

At least he didn't have to bother going inside to inquire at the official reception desk which room Ritchie was in. Hansen had sent a map to his implant that led him straight to the gardens that were outside the room she shared with Moreau.

He knew he had the right place when he saw Feena lingering in one of the two open doorways. She saw him coming and gave him a look of pity that made his heart stop. What had happened? Hansen had just pinged him. What could possibly have changed so soon?

Then he reached the doorway and realized what that pitying look had been for. It wasn't that Ritchie's condition had suddenly gone downhill.

No, something far worse was going on. Finn was sitting on the edge of Ritchie's bed, her hand in his, and his mouth on hers.

At first he thought time had frozen. But no. He could feel the breeze still blowing. Time was passing.

It just kept going on and on, that kiss.

He felt Feena's hand on his shoulder, holding him back from charging into that room. He tore his eyes away from the bed to exchange a glance with her.

She looked so sad. Like what her brother was doing actually upset her.

Then she just slipped past him towards the hedges without saying a word, her fingers trailing over to the back of his shoulder before breaking contact all together.

And Fitz looked up to see Guy Travert directly across from him in the opposite doorway. He had a bundle of flowers in his hand, a riot of jewel-tone colors that were nothing like the blooms that grew locally, but a perfect match to all the bouquets that packed the room already.

But that hand was dangling at his side, the bundle slipping from his fingers to fall to the hallway floor.

Their eyes met for just a moment. As much as Fitz had never particularly liked Guy, it was gut-wrenching, the look in his eyes. Fitz tried to raise a hand, motioning desperately for him to stay. But Guy just sadly shook his head, looked briefly towards Moreau, then turned and disappeared from the doorway.

Fitz started to run after him, as much as that would mean first awkwardly darting across the hospital room. But Finn was suddenly in front of him like a big, unmoveable wall. The corners of his mouth were barely upturned, but the whole glow of his face was one of pure triumph.

He put a hand on Fitz's shoulder, much as his sister had just done. Then he leaned in and whispered, "you should thank me."

Fitz stood there sputtering for far too long. By the time his hands were curling into fists, Finn was already gone, disappearing into the hedges after his sister. Fitz could probably catch up with him easily enough.

But Ritchie was looking at him as if he had somehow betrayed her, and he didn't know what to do with that.

Moreau had gotten up from her bed and was sitting on the edge of Ritchie's, an arm around her shoulders although she barely looked capable of supporting herself at the moment. Ritchie had her head down, both hands curled and pressed to her temples. Fitz could tell she was trying to communicate with Guy. She was using her implant. That's how desperate she was.

But from the hitching of her breath, he gathered it wasn't going well.

Moreau looked up and saw Fitz standing there. She shook her head ever so slightly, and Fitz nodded his understanding. Moreau wanted him to leave the two of them alone, at least until Ritchie had her emotions back under control.

He spun on his heel, tearing off in the direction he was sure the Berwegers had gone.

He was pretty confident around the first few turnings of the hedge maze. He could still smell Feena's scent on the air, like it was leading him on.

But he wasn't thinking about Feena. His thoughts were all throbbing with anger at Finn for what he had just done.

And every step increased the feeling that he was running away from Ritchie when he really wanted to be doing the opposite. What must she be feeling now? Just barely out of a coma, and Finn hits her with a full whammy.

And she must've felt like that was a little bit about getting at Fitz, to judge by the look she had shot his way.

Had it been?

No, if anything, it had been about getting rid of Guy, who was a much bigger part of Ritchie's life now. Getting at Fitz was just a bonus.

Fitz realized he had lost Feena's scent, and now he had no idea where they had gone or even where he was. He turned to try retracing his steps. But rather than finding his way back to the hospital, he wound up instead alone in a hedge-lined courtyard with Guy.

Guy was just standing there in the middle of a small but immaculate lawn of grass. He was looking down at his open hands as if asking them what they had done.

No, he was probably just messaging with his implant, Fitz told himself.

"Guy," Fitz said, as he stepped out onto the lawn. Guy jumped then turned to stare at him with glassy eyes. "You must know that wasn't anything Ritchie wanted. Come on. You *must* know that."

"I know full well how Murdina feels about Finn," Guy said bitterly.

"Better than me," Fitz said amiably.

"Maybe not," Guy conceded, his voice softening. "Sorry. I didn't mean to snap."

"Hey. The Berwegers do that to the best of us, trust me," Fitz said. "Come on. I was just heading back to the room. Why don't we walk back together?"

"I'm not going back there," Guy said, as if Fitz had just suggested something they both knew was impossible. Like they both jump up from the lawn they were standing on straight up into orbit.

"I know you're shaken up, but you've had a moment to get over it," Fitz said. "Ritchie needs you."

"It's not meant to be," Guy said. "I really have to go."

"You are being unbelievably stupid right now, you know that?" Fitz said. There, let Guy soak in a little of Fitz's overflowing anger. He had enough leftover for self-loathing, anyway.

"Excuse me?" Guy said.

"You can't just walk away. Like this? Come on, that's beneath even you," Fitz said.

"Even me?" Guy said incredulously. Then he blinked. "Oh, I see. You don't like me."

"I've never liked you," Fitz said amiably.

"Thanks, man," Guy said sarcastically.

"Don't take it personally. I never knew you. Not more than someone to nod to at parties," Fitz said. "But Ritchie knows you. I'm pretty sure she loves you. And you're running away?"

"Don't make it sound like that," Guy said.

"What's it like, then?" Fitz asked, still speaking almost jocularly.

"You know what it's like," Guy said. "People like you and the Berwegers live for this stuff. Old family machinations, such fun, never mind who else gets ground up in the gears."

"Like Ritchie," Fitz said pointedly.

"Yeah, well, there's nothing I can do to save Ritchie," Guy said. And Fitz realized with a start that Guy must have done something to try. What had that been? Trying to convince her to leave Fitz and the Berwegers behind? But that would mean leaving all of foreign service behind. She would never agree to that.

Guy gave Fitz a quick glance, but it was enough to see in his eyes that Fitz was right. That was exactly what Guy had tried to do. And it had turned out just as Fitz guessed.

"You can't save Ritchie, but you can save yourself," Fitz said slowly, speaking his thoughts as they formed. Then he quickly added, "I don't blame you. Truly I don't. And for what it's worth, I don't live for this stuff either."

"No, I don't really think you do," Guy agreed with a heavy sigh.

"But you can't get out. It's family. With Ritchie, she's choosing not to escape. And I just have to face that."

"This is you facing things?" Fitz asked.

"It has to be like this," Guy said. "I can't do it if I have to look at her when I tell her it's over. I suppose that sounds very cowardly to you."

"I think it does to you, too," Fitz said. "So what's going on?"

"I kind of knew this was coming," Guy said. "I've been hearing a lot from Finn Berweger. I thought I could just dismiss it all as empty threats. I could let it slide past me like Ritchie does. But he's threatening my family. All of them, even my most distant relations. And I know he means it, and he can do everything he says."

"And you can't fight back?" Fitz asked.

"Dude, I'm nineteen," Guy said. "I know that doesn't enter into the minds of either you or Ritchie, but it does to me. I'm not remotely qualified to go toe to toe with that guy and all the power his family puts behind him. If it were just me and my future on the line, maybe I'd try. But I can't risk everything my family has built on the skills of one nineteen-year-old who's still in university. I don't know enough to protect all my family's interests. He absolutely would destroy us."

"Guy, this is going to destroy her," Fitz said. It was all he had left to say.

Guy gave him a wavering smile that wouldn't hold. "I guess it's a good thing she has you then, huh?"

Before Fitz could come up with a response, Guy was already gone, lost in the hedges that had already swallowed up the Berwegers.

Fitz sighed, then summoned up a map to guide him out of the maze. But along with the map, he brought up a message from Colonel Hansen that had him swearing to himself out loud.

There had been a term of his second detention he hadn't been paying attention to when chief inspector Kasteler had explained it to him, but now that he was reading the specifics from Hansen, it flooded back to him.

When he had violated the parole on his implant, she had been compelled by law to contact his birth parents. She had done so, even before he had settled back into his detention room.

And now Colonel Hansen was sending him the details of his own conversation with Fitz's father. Fitz would be returning to Oymyakon with Ritchie and Moreau in the morning. But his father would be meeting him at the station outside the academy. Apparently, this was closer to wherever he was, finishing up whatever secret mission had kept him away.

As much as Fitz had wanted to face his father and ask him all the thousands of questions that plagued his mind, this wasn't how he wanted to do it. Particularly if Fitz's criminal charges had interfered with a mission. Fitz scanned the message again, but he couldn't tell if it had wrapped up at a really convenient time, or if someone had gotten a message through to him and he had aborted his mission early.

But as intimidating as the prospect was of facing his father at his angriest, it was also a relief. This would all be over soon.

One way or another, it would all be over.

25

RITCHIE WAS cold from the minute she stepped on board the intergalactic railway train that would be taking her back to Oymyakon. It was more than being in a cool interior, away from the hot sun and warm breezes of Braga. It was a deeper cold that settled in her bones before she'd even found her way to the sleeper compartment the three of them would be sharing, being the only cadets going back so late.

She stashed her bag, then slid into the table under the window to look out at the greenery one last time. She was just starting to wonder where she'd lost Moreau while she had gone to talk with Hansen, when the door to the sleeper compartment slid open and Moreau came in with a super-sized covered drink in each hand.

"I had to jog to the far end of the station to get these," she said as she sat down across from Ritchie and slid one of the cups over to her. Ritchie lifted the lid and instantly knew what it was when the rich caramel mell rushed up at her.

"Uber coffee bomb!" Ritchie said. "I had no idea they had these here. We could've been having them all week!"

"And they would've had to roll us back onto the train," Moreau said. She held up her cup and Ritchie did the same, tapping them together before they each took their first sip.

It didn't remove it entirely, but the rich, highly caffeinated warmth went a long way towards dispelling the cold in her bones.

"Where's Fitz? It's almost time to go," Ritchie said, frowning as she tried to angle her field of view out the window. But she could only see a tiny sliver of the platform, and what she could see was all empty space.

"Probably giving his girlfriend a long kiss goodbye," Moreau said.

"Don't say that," Ritchie said.

"Which part?" Moreau said, genuinely confused.

"Any of it," Ritchie said, flopping back into her seat with a sigh. "Anyway, I doubt he's anywhere near Feena. He probably waited until the last minute to turn in his school selection."

"Says the girl who waited to the penultimate minute," Fitz said as he came in and slid the door shut behind him.

"So you both finally picked?" Moreau said.

Ritchie and Fitz nodded, but didn't look at each other.

"Well, spill. I'm dying to know. I'm going to be on my own next year, aren't I? Go ahead and tell me," Moreau said.

"The first thing we're going to fix when we get here is the divide between the schools," Ritchie said, grabbing Moreau's hand and giving it a squeeze. "I know you'll have to study, but we're still going to hang out."

"Oh, I have no doubt about that," Moreau said, quirking a single eyebrow. "You're going to want to help me with all my homework. I just know it."

"She'll get vicarious thrills assisting in your research," Fitz said, but it was a half-hearted teasing. He was leaning against the door, arms crossed, not joining them at the table, and he sounded distracted.

"I'm not going to pretend that's not all true," Ritchie said. "But yes, it's guardian school for me."

"Zahnd will be so pleased when she hears," Moreau said with just a hint of jealousy.

"She was," Ritchie admitted.

"You told her first?" Moreau said.

"Only because she was there with Kasteler when I went to the offi-cers' lounge in the station to tell Colonel Hansen," Ritchie said. "And it was just before I got on the train, so she only knew a few minutes before you did. Honest."

"Kasteler came to say goodbye to Hansen?" Moreau asked with a raised eyebrow.

"They were still there when I left, even though they were announcing final boarding," Ritchie said. "How much do you want to bet he'll miss the train?"

"Any amount you like," Moreau said. "There's no way he's abandoning us."

"I wonder if he'll transfer to some school on Braga for next year?" Ritchie said. "Not because of Kasteler, although I suppose that would be a bonus for him. But because of the task force. That doesn't end when we graduate from the academy, does it? We've barely achieved anything. And there's more to be done than ever."

"Wyss and Sokolov will still be there for another year," Moreau reminded her. "Maybe he has something else in mind for us."

"Well, no hurry. We have a full year left at Oymyakon," Ritchie said.

"A year left of being buddies," Moreau agreed, and they clasped hands again across the table.

The train started to move forward, leaving the station behind, then rising up into the clouds. Ritchie sighed as the last glimpse of green was obscured by a cloud bank. It would be a long year until she saw that much green again.

Ritchie and Moreau seemed to notice at the same time that Fitz was still leaning against the door with his arms crossed, staring fixedly at the floor. They exchanged a questioning look, then matching shrugs. Neither of them had any idea why he was being so sullen.

"I suppose I don't even have to ask which school you picked?" Moreau asked, but there was just a hint of hopefulness in her tone. Ritchie felt bad. Moreau really didn't want to end up alone at that cold school.

"Guardian," Fitz said, but automatically, as if he were only half listening.

"Hey, Fitz, I was just teasing before," Moreau said. "But it was unkind. I shouldn't have said a thing."

"What?" Fitz asked, finally looking up at the two of them.

"About kissing Feena goodbye. It wasn't funny and is none of my business. Sorry," Moreau said.

"Oh. I didn't hear you," Fitz said. "It doesn't matter. I haven't seen Feena since she was in your hospital room yesterday."

Then he lapsed back into preoccupation, head down as he studied the floor.

Moreau looked across the table at Ritchie, but Ritchie just shrugged again. She had no idea what was going on with Fitz. As usual.

"I'm going to find Hansen," Moreau said as she got up from the table.

"Make sure he's on the train?" Ritchie asked.

Moreau grinned at her. "Partly, sure. But I need to talk to him about a thing. Before we get to school. It'll just take a minute." Then she glanced over at Fitz, then back at Ritchie. "Or two."

Ritchie glared at her furiously. This was obviously Moreau getting out of the way so Ritchie could be alone with Fitz, but that was the last thing she wanted. Another long conversation about how he couldn't tell her anything? No, thank you.

But there was no stopping Moreau when she was on a mission. She just gave Ritchie an apologetic smile, then moved Fitz out of her way so she could slip out the door and into the corridor.

As soon as Moreau was gone, Fitz just fell back into place against the door. Ritchie slowly sipped the rest of her uber coffee bomb and watched the sky out the window go from deep indigo to black as they reached the level of orbit where they were going to dock with the jump drive ring.

Fitz finally slumped into the seat across from her, but he still didn't say anything.

"You're really going to make me ask, aren't you?" Ritchie said when she couldn't take the silence anymore.

"What? No. I just have a lot on my mind. I don't need you to ask me anything," Fitz said.

"Are you mad at me?" Ritchie asked.

"Because of what Finn did?" Fitz asked incredulously.

Ritchie practically rocked back in her seat at that. "No, that was probably the last thing on my mind."

"Good. I mean, it ought to be. I know that was just Finn being Finn," Fitz said. He gave up with a frustrated sigh. If he felt like he was talking himself into a corner, Ritchie couldn't blame him. Just the thought that he would blame her for what Finn did was increasing her heart rate.

Or maybe that was the caffeine. Ritchie pushed the empty cup away from her and crossed her arms to resume glaring out the window. But there was nothing out there but stars and blackness now.

But she couldn't match him for aloofness. There was no point in trying. So she said, "I meant, are you mad at me for choosing the guardian school? I know you really wanted the two of us to be a working diplomat/guardian pair."

Fitz sighed, then started rubbing at an invisible flaw on the table-top. "I did when I was a kid before I knew better. But you said that wasn't what you wanted. You said that a year ago. I haven't given it a thought since."

"Haven't you?" Ritchie said skeptically. Then she swallowed hard. He was probably being honest. Because the distance between them had suddenly appeared the very day they had had that conversation.

She was *not* going to start thinking that was her fault.

But Fitz just shrugged, his eyes still on the flaw he was attempting to buff out with the side of his thumb. "We'll still be at the same school next year. I'm not disappointed about that."

"Poor Moreau," Ritchie said. But her sadness extended to herself as well. She was going to miss her buddy.

"She won't be alone," Fitz told her. "Janelle Frei and Kye Imhof will both be with her."

"I didn't know that," Ritchie said. "That's two more buddy pairs splitting. I guess everything is coming to an end."

"Sure, after another year at Oymyakon," Fitz said with the smallest of smiles.

"Right. I'm getting maudlin too soon," Ritchie said.

"Just a touch," he said.

They were quiet again for another spell, but this was more like a lull in conversation with a closeness still between them. Not like most of the last year.

But Ritchie had to say the very worst thing. She couldn't not say it. "Are you sad because of leaving Feena behind again?" He looked up at her, startled, and she felt her cheeks heating, but she plowed on. "It's not the weirdest thing in the world if, after spending months together because Hansen wanted you to spy on her, that you… I don't know. Got used to her?"

Fitz laughed. "That's the kindest way to put it, isn't it?"

"Well, is it true?" Ritchie asked, her cheeks still flaming too hotly.

"No," Fitz said. But then he reassessed and said, "okay, I did get used to her, as you say. But nothing more than that. I'm not sorry to leave her behind, anymore than you're sorry to leave Finn behind." He was focused on the tabletop again, but he glanced up at her through that lock of hair that always fell over his face to see her response to that.

"I'm the farthest thing from sorry on that score," Ritchie assured him. "I still can't get Guy to answer any of my messages."

"Well, I'm sorry about that," Fitz said. "I caught up with him after he ran off, yesterday. But I couldn't convince him to come back."

"What did he say?" Ritchie asked, although she wasn't sure she wanted to know.

Fitz sighed again. "Basically, Finn is never going to leave you alone, and Guy doesn't want to get in his way. Apparently Finn has been threatening to ruin the Traverts politically and financially, and Guy believes he will do as he says."

"I'm sure he'll try," Ritchie said darkly.

Fitz gave a humorless laugh. "I would say the same. Bring it on, right? But Guy says that's what makes him different from you and I. He doesn't want to risk anything."

"That's *not* what he said," Ritchie said firmly.

"Well, close enough," Fitz said. "Look, give him a little time and space, and then message him again. I don't think he's ever going to change his mind about your relationship being over, but I'm sure once he feels calmer and safer, he'll at least talk to you. Maybe explain himself a little."

"You think so?" Ritchie asked.

"I do," Fitz said.

"I guess that's what I'll do," Ritchie said. Then it was her turn to heave a sigh. "That will be easier once we get back to school. It's just being here with nothing to do but stew about it that I can't stop messaging him. Once we get back and I start drowning in assignments, I'll forget to message him again, just like last year." It was getting hard to get words out past the lump in her throat. "He's probably better off without me tying him down but never being there, anyway."

"For what it's worth, I don't think Guy would agree with that," Fitz said, shooting her another quick glance.

"Well, I do," Ritchie said.

There was another long silence, but this time it was Fitz that spoke first. "As to getting back to school, I wanted to talk to you about that."

"About school?" Ritchie asked, surprised. "You never want to talk about school."

"It's more about missing school," he admitted with a wry grin.

"What's going on?" she asked him, narrowing her eyes at him.

"When we get back to Oymyakon, my father is going to be waiting for me at the station," Fitz admitted.

"This is why you've been acting so weird?" Ritchie asked, everything suddenly clicking into place. He nodded. "Missing school… you mean he's taking you away?"

"I'll be going back to Buennagel with him for a time, yes," Fitz said. "Colonel Hansen already knows. But there's more."

"What's that?" Ritchie asked.

Fitz took a deep breath, then finally looked up at her, really made eye contact with her. "I want you to come with me."

"Back to Buennagel?" Ritchie asked. The words coming out of her mouth didn't feel real.

"Back to Buennagel," Fitz agreed. "That's where we need to be. That's where I can finally tell you everything."

Ritchie was too overwhelmed to form words, but she was sure her enthusiastic nodding communicated her feelings more than well enough.

26

FITZ WOKE FAR TOO EARLY the next morning, unable to sleep through the jostling of entering the Oymyakon atmosphere. He slipped out of his bunk as silently as he could so he wouldn't wake either Ritchie or Moreau, picking up his boots and carrying them with him as he crept out of the sleeper car.

The intergalactic railway train was just as he remembered it. The sounds of their car's steward working in the little kitchenette and storage area off the main corridor echoed strangely to his ears. The pressure changes from space to atmosphere always took some time to settle out, and his ears were struggling with it at the moment. It sounded like he was underwater, but that muffling, distancing feeling just matched his mood.

He slipped on his boots, then walked as far aft along the train as he could go to stand in the glass-sided observation car. The storms of Oymyakon whipped around the train all around him, lightning forking over distant mountaintops while the closer rain streaked across the glass.

He wondered if this was the same observation car he had been in the first time he had come to Oymyakon. The one where he and Ritchie had seen the body of the Feltzkinder caught in the train's wake. Probably not. It was probably just another of the same model.

But maybe it was.

He walked all the way to the back of the car to press his forehead against the glass. As if that cold rush could calm his furious thoughts.

He heard soft footsteps coming up behind him, then Moreau was standing beside him, hands in her pockets as she mimicked his posture against the glass.

"I came here to be alone," he told her, but he wasn't irritated.

"I figured," Moreau said. "I also figured you've had enough of that. So, tough."

"Always such empathy from you," Fitz said.

"This is some of my best work here," she said. Then she pivoted her head to look over at him without lifting her forehead off of the glass. "What are you stewing over now?"

"The usual," he said.

"I bet I know," Moreau said, turning back to look at the rocky valley rolling away behind them.

"What's that?" Fitz asked despite himself.

"You're wondering if deep down Ritchie didn't enjoy that kiss," Moreau said, giving him an evil grin.

"I am not."

"Because it certainly looked like she wasn't fighting it, right?"

"I wasn't thinking about that," Fitz growled.

"But you are now," Moreau said.

"What are you doing here?" Fitz asked.

"Making you confront some things," Moreau said. "So tell me what you think. Did she?"

Fitz bit down on his tongue, swearing to himself he wouldn't answer. Then he said, "no more than I do when Feena kisses me."

"Sure," Moreau said, as if that was the answer she had expected. "Just exactly that amount."

"Exactly," Fitz said.

"Just exactly that non-zero amount."

"Shut up, you," he said.

"Hey, you shouldn't feel bad on either score, is all I'm saying. You'd have to be made of stone to be unmoved," Moreau said. "It's just biology. Or, in their case, super-biology."

"It doesn't mean anything," Fitz said.

"Exactly," Moreau said.

"Did you come all the way back here at this hour just to irritate me?" Fitz asked.

"No," Moreau said. "I've been talking with Colonel Hansen."

"Not about that," Fitz said, appalled at the thought.

"Of course not," Moreau said. "We were talking about your father."

"What about my father?" Fitz asked.

"I know he's meeting you at the station," Moreau said. "He's arranged to take you away from the school for an indeterminate amount of time."

"I'll be coming back," Fitz said. "If that's what's worrying you."

"I know you talked to Hansen about taking Ritchie with you," Moreau said.

"Like I said, it's just for a few days," Fitz said.

"Well, here's what you don't know," Moreau said, pushing away from the glass and turning to face him. Reluctantly, he did the same. "I'm coming too."

"No, you're not," Fitz said, but even as he said the words, he had a sneaking suspicion they weren't going to turn out to be true.

"There's more," Moreau said, her eyebrows up as she waited for him to ask what she meant.

"Hansen is coming too?" Fitz guessed.

"No, of course not. He has classes," she said.

"So, what then?" Fitz asked.

"Sokolov and Wyss are coming too," Moreau said with a grin.

"What? Why?"

"Well, I was talking to Hansen about what the task force is going to do next year with us split between two planets and three schools. And he saw an opportunity in this unscheduled trip to arrange a secret meeting."

"Wait, you're serious?" Fitz said.

"I'm always serious," Moreau said. "I know we're going to Buennagel and not Jorda, but Buennagel is still a central planet. And lots of people stop by on business to see someone as important as your father. One of his guests while we're all there is going to be someone Hansen wants us to meet."

"He already planned for this?" Fitz asked.

"Even while the three of us were wondering what we'd be doing next year, Hansen already had it all figured out. He just hadn't told us yet. Our work on Braga is going to be even more important than our work on Oymyakon. But we still need a handler."

"And we're going to meet this person at my parents' house?" Fitz asked. Moreau nodded. Fitz just shook his head disbelievingly. "You know, I already had a lot of major stuff to deal with on this trip. I don't think I needed another."

"You're planning to tell her?" Moreau asked, so excited she practically rose up on her tiptoes.

"After I talk to my father, I'm telling her," Fitz said.

Then he had to endure Moreau throwing her arms around him and squeezing him tight. She had a surprising amount of strength considering her size, and Fitz had to catch his breath again after she let him go.

"Finally," Moreau said happily. "Finally, this will all be over."

"I hope she's as happy about it as you are," Fitz said.

"Well, I doubt that will be her reaction," Moreau said. "She's definitely going to be angry first. But you always knew that. You know you did. But eventually, eventually, she's going to be glad you told her."

"I hope so," Fitz said, and put his forehead back on the glass.

The rain outside the windows turned to snow as the antigravity disks carried the train up the side of a mountain in a serpentine track. He glanced over at the map displayed on the arm of the nearest chair. They were skirting an entire mountain range to avoid a raging blizzard, but that would only delay them a few hours.

By lunchtime, he'd be facing his father for the first time in more months than he could count.

But in a lot of ways, he'd be facing his father for the first time, full stop. It would be the first time when Fitz knew just who he was and what he wanted. He had that fixed very firmly in his mind. His father in his mind had morphed from an indomitable force to be thwarted at all times to something else entirely. Something more human, but still a force to be respected if not feared.

Moreau didn't say a word as they gazed out over the bleak landscape, but she slipped her hand into his and gave it a squeeze. It was all the reminder he needed.

He wasn't doing it alone. As overwhelming and frightening as his father could be, this time Fitz was ready to face him.

Because this time, he had allies.

CHECK OUT BOOK SIX

The Ritchie and Fitz Sci-Fi Murder Mysteries will continue with Book Six, A Lethal Betrayal.

Murdina Ritchie left her childhood home of Buennagel when a volatile, very alien species abducted her father during a failed diplomatic meeting. Six years later, she finds herself flying back. Her best friend Shackleton Fitz IV needs her help.

His father's increasingly bizarre behavior demands an explanation. And Ritchie and Fitz specialize in finding explanations.

But when another guest at the house dies when brutally attacked their first night home, Ritchie and Fitz find themselves caught up in two cases. Someone in the house is the killer, and anyone in the house could be next.

A Lethal Betrayal, Book 6 and the concluding chapter in the Ritchie and Fitz Sci-Fi Murder Mysteries.

NEW SERIES: THE FORGOTTEN PLANET

Coming soon from Ratatoskr Press Books, the new YA sci-fi series *The Forgotten Planet* starts with book 1: *Raiding the Forgotten Derelict*.

History sleeps beneath them all, but only she sees it.

Lafayette Eloi always knew her parents thought differently from others. They kept their books buried beneath her mother's house. They spoke an old language in the dead of night, whispering behind closed doors and bolted shutters. She grew up in a village where no one was related to her, and she never knew why.

Then, after her mother died, her father came to fetch her. Now she and her mother's dog assist her father in his work. The work discussed in whispers in the dark. The work that had cost Lafayette so much all her young life.

But now she learns just how much her father's work means to their entire world. Only no one knows anything about it. Only her father. And only Lafayette.

Because the work that consumed her father's entire life and her mother's too now nibbles at the fringe's of Lafayette's own life. And she cannot refuse its call.

Raiding the Forgotten Derelict, first book in the new YA sci-fu series *The Forgotten Planet,* available in September 2024 from Ratatoskr Press Books.

COMPLETE SERIES: THE RITCHIE AND FITZ SCI-FI MURDER MYSTERIES

The Ritchie and Fitz Sci-Fi Murder Mysteries starts with *Murder on the Intergalactic Railway.*

For Murdina Ritchie, acceptance at the Oymyakon Foreign Service Academy means one last chance at her dream of becoming a diplomat for the Union of Free Worlds. For Shackleton Fitz IV, it represents his last chance not to fail out of military service entirely.

Strange that fate should throw them together now, among the last group of students admitted after the start of the semester. They had once shared the strongest of friendships. But that all ended a long time ago.

But when an insufferable but politically important woman turns up murdered, the two agree to put their differences aside and work together to solve the case.

Because the murderer might strike again. But more importantly, solving a murder would just have to impress the dour colonel who clearly thinks neither of them belong at his academy.

Murder on the Intergalactic Railway, the first book in *The Ritchie and Fitz Sci-Fi Murder Mysteries.*

COMPLETE SERIES: THE TRAVELS OF SCOUT SHANNON

The complete six-book series *The Travels of Scout Shannon* begin with book one, *Under Falling Skies*.

Scout Shannon's whole family died the day the Space Farers dropped an asteroid on their domed city. Now she lives alone, out in the wild with only her dogs for company. She prefers it that way.

But Scout finds herself at a crossroads. One road leads back to a quiet life snug under the protective dome of a city. The other road leads to a life in the rebellion, a life of adventure and excitement but also danger. Dare she try to find the rebels hiding in the hills?

Then a chance encounter with a stranger from the other side of the galaxy threatens to derail what remains of Scout's life. The entire galaxy awaits her, if she survives the next four days.

Under Falling Skies, a young adult science fiction novel, set on a remote planet with a distinctly Old West feel. For fans of gunslinging women and young girl assassins. And dogs.

Under Falling Skies, the first book in *The Travels of Scout Shannon*, available everywhere now.

SCI-FI SERIAL PODCAST!

Check out my new monthly podcast of serialized science fiction: THE TALES OF THE CHAI MAKHANI TRIO!

Elyot loathes the massive Commonwealth ships that hover menacingly over his home world of Adghal. He hates the Commonwealth enforcers who harass the populace even more. But with his mother missing and presumed dead, Elyot keeps his head down and strives to avoid notice. And he succeeds until the day two strangers enter his life...

New episodes of this sci-fi serial drop every 1st of the month.

Now streaming on all major podcast platforms. Also available in eBook and print everywhere books or sold. For a complete episode listing, check out the page on my website.

ALSO FROM RATATOSKR PRESS

Also from Ratatoskr Press, *The Witches Three Cozy Mystery Series* by Cate Martin, a mix of mystery and magic that begins with Book 1: *Charm School*.

Amanda Clarke thinks of herself as perfectly ordinary in every way. Just a small-town girl who serves breakfast all day in a little diner nestled next to the highway, nothing but dairy farms for miles around. She fits in there.

But then an old woman she never met dies, and Amanda was named in her will. Now Amanda packs a bag and heads to the big city, to Miss Zenobia Weekes' Charm School for Exceptional Young Ladies. And it's not in just any neighborhood. No, she finds herself on Summit Avenue in St. Paul, a street lined with gorgeous old houses, the former homes of lumber barons, railroad millionaires, even the writer F. Scott Fitzgerald. Why, Amanda can practically hear the jazz music still playing across the decades.

Scratch that. The music really, literally, still plays in the backyard of the charm school. Because the house stretches across time itself. Without a witch to protect this tear in the fabric of the world, anything can spill over. Like music.

Or like murder.

The complete series is out now, and it all starts with *Charm School*.

FREE EBOOK!

Like exclusive, free content?

To get two prequel short stories to THE RITCHIE AND FITZ SCI-FI MURDER MYSTERIES as well as a bonus prequel novelette to the completed six-book series THE TRAVELS OF SCOUT SHANNON, signup for my monthly newsletter at KateMacLeodWrites.com.

Thank you!

ABOUT THE AUTHOR

Photograph © 2016 Jonathan Conklin

Kate MacLeod has written stories which have appeared in *Analog, Strange Horizons* and *Mythic Delirium,* among other places. She is also the author of two young adult science fictions series: *The Travels of Scout Shannon,* and *The Ritchie and Fitz Sci-Fi Murder Mysteries.* She also contributes to a serialized science fiction podcast called *The Tales of the Chai Makhani Trio.* She currently lives in Minneapolis, Minnesota.

Find out more about the author and sign up for her newsletter at KateMacLeodWrites.com.

ALSO BY KATE MACLEOD

Novels

The Slums of the Solar System:

Mitwa

The Mars of Malcontents

The Whole World for Each

Books 1-3 Box Set

The Travels of Scout Shannon:

Under Falling Skies

In Quaking Hills

Among Treacherous Stars

Against Impassable Barriers

Over Freezing Altitudes

At Galactic Central

The Travels of Scout Shannon Books 1-3

The Travels of Scout Shannon Books 4-6

The Travels of Scout Shannon Books 1-6

The Ritchie and Fitz Sci-Fi Murder Mysteries:

Murder on the Intergalactic Railway

Murder in the Skies

Body in the Catacombs

Death on the Summit

An Undiplomatic Murder

A Lethal Betrayal

The Forgotten Planet

Raiding the Forgotten Derelict (Forthcoming September 2024)

Sci-Fi Novellas

The Intergenerational Tree

I Rise into a Daybreak

Caper Novellas

The Third Pole Job

The Twelve Days of Christmas Job

10-Story Collections

Tales of Blood and Ink

Tales of Old Gods and New

5-Story Collections

Tales from Heian-Kyo and Others

Tales from the Edges and Ends

Tales from Forgotten Days

Tales from Ancient and Future Times

Tales from Across Space

www.ingramcontent.com/pod-product-compliance
Lightning Source LLC
Chambersburg PA
CBHW030622190726
48286CB00008B/2353